S0-CJP-010

REGARDS, RODEO
The Mariner Dog of Cassis

Alan Armstrong
Illustrated by Martha Armstrong

J. N. Townsend Publishing
Exeter, New Hampshire
1999

Copyright © 1999. Alan Armstrong.
Illustrations copyright © 1999. Martha Armstrong.
All rights reserved.
Cover and text design by Design Point, Epping, NH.

Printed in Canada

Published by J. N. Townsend Publishing
12 Greenleaf Drive
Exeter, New Hampshire 03833
800/333-9883
www.jntownsendpublishing.com

Library of Congress Cataloging-in-Publication Data

Armstrong, Alan (Alan W.), 1939-
Regards, Rodeo / Alan Armstrong.
p. cm.
1. Dogs--France--Cassis--Fiction. 2. Dogs--Massachusetts--Fiction. I. Title.

PS3551.R4667 R44 1999
813'.54--dc21 99-046029

ISBN: 1-880158-25-6

To Faith.
To Al and Jo.

Prologue

A year ago my wife got a grant to paint for a semester in France, and I went along. I met a remarkable dog there who became my friend. I encouraged his correspondence with my dog back home. There was of course some explaining to do to our son who was taking care of the home dog. These are letters between Rodeo, a dog in Cassis, France, and Jefe, my dog in Hatfield, Massachusetts, and a few between my son Benjamin and me.

There is a dog named Rodeo in Cassis, and a dog named Jefe in Hatfield. The people they describe exist and some of the facts of their lives are part of this story. As for the War, it was as it was.

I'eu, d'uno Chato enamourado
Aro Qu'ai di la Mar—parado,
Cantarai, se Diéu voù, un Enfant de Cassis,
Un simple pescaire di' anchoio
Qu emé soun gämbié me sa voio
Dou pur amour gagné li joio. . .

Frederic Mistral, "Calendau," 1867

[I'll sing, if it is God's will,
About a child of Cassis, a simple fisher of anchovies
Who by grace and will has realized
The joys, the realm, the beauty of love...]

April 20, Cassis

My Dear Monsieur Jefe—

I write you as a messenger. Please pretend that as a dog strange to you and intending no hostility, I turn my head aside and allow the usual sniffs of investigation. As our Voltaire has said, "The superfluous is the most necessary commodity." In the matter of scent, what is superfluous to me is very important to you. Which does not mean I am indifferent to what my scent conveys; I have contrived it with as much art as any *femme fatale*, as I'm sure you have worked up yours. And so, with the preliminaries accomplished and the wags of curiosity commenced, let me tell you about our life here.

My name is Rodeo. I am what is called here a *berger*—a shepherd dog. I am tall and sand colored, my ears are black and pointed, I have fine walnut eyes and a black star on my forehead. Those who admire me say that I am handsome, if a bit fierce. I like it that I look fierce, but I am not mean. I do not bite—oh a nip sometimes, the snap when I need to remind or to command respect. My tail is fine and bushy, set high like a fox's. I am fit. Although I am well past the middle of my age you can see the lines of my ribs. I live in Cassis, a small French fishing village near Marseille on the Mediterranean.

Your *patron* Alan is here. He comes to see me in the morning before I start work. He calls me "The Mariner" and tells me things he does not say to people. I tell my patron that we dogs are like priests, we are confessors. What does a priest do that dogs do not do? Jean-Michel shakes his head and says that I have not yet grown into my understanding. For my part I think they sometimes over-value their understandings. It blinds them to how things are.

I work with Jean-Michel in the sailing school. He is very correct, firm to a point of fierceness if you do not know him, but we talk about all of life. He told me about a German poet who did not like dogs because we have no conversation and so cannot express our feelings.

"What do you think of that?" *le patron* asked. "No conversation in the attitude, the scent, the stance, the voice?"

"That man is a fool!"

"No, but he is ignorant. Most people don't realize that dogs have conversation. They think because dogs do not fight wars of religion they are stupid."

We work on the port with the *Classes de Mer de Cassis*. Our *bureau* is behind the boatyard, but mostly we are on

the water. Jean-Michel is Master of the School.

For all I call him *le patron,* I am his guardian, his protector. When he is around I am not distracted by anything—not even by the lovely Obsidienne or the comely Gigi. Only when he is absent do I relax. But soon I begin to worry for his return.

Alan calls me The Mariner, but with Jean-Michel and everyone else my name is Rodeo. *Le patron* cannot pronounce a sharp "R," so when he calls me it sounds like "Hrrodeo." He learned my name from a Western. Is Rodeo the name of a brave horse? Tell me about the film if you know it. I should like to observe my namesake.

I was trained as a sheep dog but I have never herded sheep. All my work has been at the sailing school. I herd *les petits marins* and their boats. I ride standing up in *Zodiac,* which is *le patron*'s rubber boat. I like to ride up front with my nose in the wind and my paws on the prow.

We look dashing at sea. *Le patron* sits strong as a barrel at the engine which he runs full-out with one arm on the tiller and the other on the gunnel. I stand at the front breasting the wind. The spray and swells do not bother me, but when the sea is rough *le patron* makes me lie down. I have to lie in the bilge water then. I do not like that.

I am a good sailor. No matter how heavy the sea I

never fall in. But when one of the children goes overboard I jump in and bark loudly to help *le patron* find the child. My barking gives the young one courage. I am a strong swimmer, so I let the child cling to me. I know he won't sink. They all wear the regulation orange life vests. They couldn't go under if they wanted to. Many children have fallen into the sea, but we have never had a drowning in our school.

I am famous for my bark. That is what drew Alan to me. He heard me barking morning after morning, heard the weather and the excitement in it, the urging. He came to make my acquaintance. He was very formal. He came over and asked *le patron* if he could make my acquaintance. Through him we introduced. That is the way it is here. Most French dogs will not speak to strangers.

My bark carries in the wind. Some of the citizens complain that my bark is annoying. *Le patron* explains that I am a *berger*, I am doing the work of a *berger* herding the sailboats. It is like people talking at their work. It is a necessary thing.

I have strengthened my voice in the manner of the opera singers Pavarotti and Domingo who come here for their exercises. It begins low in my belly. I bark because *le patron* is excited and I am excited for the children. I bark to accompany their high squeals and screams when *le patron* cheers them in the race with his loud calls of "*Allez*! *Allez*! *Allez*!" I join him with expressions of excitement. I cannot help myself! He shouts the "Giddyup! Giddyup!" from the Westerns.

To urge them on when the race is close he yells, "*Giddyup Ongawa*!" which is African for "Go after the lion!" He got that from Tarzan. We watch Tarzans and Westerns at night. *Le patron* yells and cheers every time, but I have seen them all so often now I go to sleep.

Jean-Michel has a deep voice for commands. He talks rapidly sometimes, then slowly for emphasis. For effect he will growl or yell. He gestures with his fist in the air when he yells the "*Giddyup Ongawa*!"

I have trained my bark after his way of command. I have a four-beat bark for my commands, five beats for matters of urgency. My working voice is high like the tenor Domingo's. I am proud that

it carries. Gigi and Obsidienne listen for it and they are glad to hear me at my work. Like M'sieur Pavarotti and M'sieur Domingo, I sing for them. They know when things are going well and they know when there is trouble. My music readies them for my other attentions. This also I have learned from our famous visitors.

I get excited when we prepare for a sail. I hate it when one of the children lags behind or forgets his life vest. He must then be sent back, and we have so little time! By noon we must be back on the port with the tackle stowed and the boats lined up. So "Hurry!" I tell them, "Hurry! We must get out to sea!" Sometimes I have to jump into the water for a quick swim or carry the buffer tire in my mouth to calm my excitement.

Barking is one of the things you learn in sheep dog school—barks of warning, barks of encouragement, barking about the weather changing, barking to keep the flock together and to let the strays know where the main pack is.

I bark when one of the sailboats strays or a youngster forgets how to tack or how to come about. Sometimes a child will lose the wind or get blown off course. Sometimes a centerboard drifts up and the little sailor cannot command his way. Once or twice a tiller has come off. I bark hard then to remind them what to do. When a tiller goes adrift I must retrieve it. It floats, so I get it in my teeth and carry it to *le patron*.

When it is time to go back to port I must command the children's attention. *Le patron* circles the fleet helping the sailors get their boats in line. Then he heaves the painter to the first boat. The first sailor must secure it to his boat, then catch and secure the painter from the second. The children often drop those lines or do not fasten them properly. Meanwhile the wind is blowing and the boats are scattering. Sometimes I am sent to carry a painter. That part of my everyday work is the hardest. The boats move in the wind and I must catch them! When they are finally tied in line together they look like chicks following the hen.

What is your training? What school did you attend? Not to be rude, but the poodles I know here are idle, trivial fellows or *bijoux* to their ladies—except the ones who travel with the gypsies to the casino, and their work is not reputable. And the way poodles are cut! Ridiculous. Alan says you are different. You must give me a picture of yourself. And you must tell me also if it is true that no poodle can be a Seeing Eye dog because of the breed's enthusiasm to please. The mongrels here snicker that a guide poodle would walk his charge into the sea if given the command "*Allez*!" But the ones who say this have no breeding, so perhaps they are envious. I cannot ask these questions of any poodle here, but in a correspondence everything is permitted.

Do you go about on a leash or are you are trained to follow? I am trained to follow, but when we leave our quarter of the port *le patron* fixes a broad red strap to my collar—leash enough to restrain a mastiff, I tell him. He does it to show off, but whether he is showing off his power or mine, I cannot tell. For Sundays there is a bright purple one. I would prefer a fine kerchief.

Speaking of Sundays, what is your faith? Are you Catholic in your family, or do you follow a *culte protestant*? We are Catholic. Jean-Michel makes a gift of his dives to the church, as I shall tell you. What is your gift?

One méchant dog here has put it out that I bark because I am afraid of the water. That is not true—it is a *canard,* as we say—and if I get the chance I'll rip his hide for his lie. I like the water. I swim every day with *le patron*. That is our bathing. *Le patron* maintains that the salt does us as well as the famous soap of Marseille, so I do not have to endure the indignity of the perfume worn by my friends who are bathed in town every week at *Le Toilettage des Chiens* next to the church.

I am the only dog on the port who works on the water. There are dogs here who ride on boats but I am the only dog in Cassis who works on the water, exposed to peril and saving lives. As

Christophe, who is Jean-Michel's assistant, puts it, "Rodeo is the first dog that is a sailing teacher!"

When we get back to port I nap in front of the office until it is time to prepare for the two o'clock class. My water dish is there. You understand that I cannot drink the water of the sea because it is salt. I drank it once as a puppy. *Le patron* said I would be sick from it, but I laughed and drank it because I was thirsty and it was water. Then of course I was sick.

The break between classes is a sweet time for me. I doze in the shade when Jean-Michel goes to the back of the tackle room for his nap. The pounding and yelling at the dry dock stills as the workers take off their work coats and find a shade for lunch. In the breeze I catch the scent of their cheeses and sausages, and then their tobaccos. Those mix with whiffs of diesel, tar, and pitch from the boats they have been repairing, and the pungence of new paint.

When the water is calm the sun draws up its fragrance—sea moss, fish, old rope, decaying hulls, the salt. When there is a land breeze I catch the faint perfumes of the grapes and smokes from the burnings. I have a friend, the horse Pierre, who tells me how lovely the fragrance of the meadow is when the grass is in bloom, how sweet the bloom of hay in his barn, but the noontime smells at the sea edge are the most beautiful to me.

About two o'clock, slowly at first like our tree crickets or *cigales* in the morning, the voices begin again, the motors, the cruisers with their loudspeakers advertising for tourists, "*Visitez Les Calanques*! *Visitez Les Calanques!*"—inviting the day guests from Marseille and Aix aboard for a ride to the deep cuts in the coast where the brave submariners used to come during the War to rescue the *maquis* and the Jews. There were shootings then, but only one of those rescue submarines was ever sunk.

What I know about you is that you are a black poodle of eleven pounds. Your hair is cut short and shines like astrakhan. Alan says you are a good jumper and runner, and that you are brave, which is your French heritage. But your name is strange to me; no dog here has such a name.

So I might judge your size Alan described how you get up to your watching place on the sofa. Five or six attempts are required before your hind paws catch on the edge so you can push yourself up. Once aboard you lie lengthwise on the arm rest.

So you may judge my size, if I were allowed on it—which I am not—I could get up on the sofa with an easy bound. I could not fit on the arm rest. I require a full seat like *le patron*.

It is a thing good to hear how you wiggle your stump tail rapidly when anyone of the family appears. Alan calls what remains of your tail your "monitor." I am not sure about the word "monitor"—does that mean your wagger or does it refer to the wag of what was your tail? Do you suffer like some amputees—a shadow of pain in the part that was cut off? It makes me shudder to think of your amputation! I think it a shame that they cut off your tail. The poodles here keep their tails and are very proud of them. For us French dogs our tails are our flags.

I am told that you have a fine smile and many expressions and tones of voice, and that you laugh, which is contrary to Aristotle who observed that only humans laugh, so so much for Aristotle. When a game of Chase begins you sneeze with excitement and begin to bark which makes everyone laugh. Your *patron* admires your understanding and your patience. He has told me about your work together in the book van. He says you have a strong bark with many shades of firmness and that you sleep in his bed.

I weigh 37 kg or, in the way you figure it, eighty pounds. I have large black calluses on both elbows from riding on the prow of *Zodiac*. From an accident on the boat my jaw shudders when I drink and it appears that my teeth are chattering, but they are not. The water spills though, which is unfortunate.

You have a scar from a knee operation? You tore your knee chasing a cat? I have heard Alan's version of this story but I must hear it from you to understand. What I want to know immediately is, Did the cat survive? Had I suffered such an injury I would have seen to the swift death of the cat. But they are said to have nine lives. Surely you took one.

I am eleven years old. *Le patron* says I have achieved my full growth and am now on the other side. When we stand together my head comes to his waist. I have been his friend since I was three weeks old. I sleep in his room.

As for *le patron*, he is a vigorous man with the body and color of one who has spent much of his life on the water. He has a large head like carved bronze. His chest is powerful from swimming, his trunk and legs slim like a boy's. His color is like shined old copper. Most days he wears bathing trunks and a T-shirt. He is the Master of the sailing school but he prefers to describe himself as a high diver.

He has a printed card with a color photograph of his dive. On the back it says *Jean-Michel Beaujon—Le Cassidain Volant'—Plongeur de Haut Vol, 32 métres de hauteur, vitesse dans l'eau 93 km/h.—* "The Flyer of Cassis, High-Diving from 90', hitting the water at 60 mph." He can show you a dossier of his dives. He does it to raise money for the handicapped. That is his gift to God.

How does Alan describe himself? What is his vocation? He goes about making notes and photographs. He asks people about their work and the equipment of their trades. He smiles at the dogs and stops to talk with any who respond. This morning when he exchanged greetings with Felix, Felix bowed in his curious way, so Alan stopped for a chat. Felix rides low to the ground, being the son of the basset bitch Cerise and a red retriever. The mistress of Felix, Mme Goncourt, found it quite peculiar to look back as she progressed in her shopping and find an unknown man of some age on his haunches addressing her dog, who was bowed down like a Mohammedan before him.

He photographs the dogs. He will kneel down suddenly in front of a cafe to get a shot. Naturally this makes the ladies uneasy as they must adjust their legs to appear graceful in the photograph. And it disturbs the dogs in their relaxation.

Does he dress with the dignity of his vocation? He is a fair and handsome man of his age, stocky, gray-haired. He appears on the port in unpressed white trousers, a freshly laundered shirt of some quality, sunglasses and a palm weave hat. On his back he wears a red pack like a German tourist. He is never without the *sac*, the camera, and a fold of paper, but he wears no jacket, no tie, and he does not carry a case. He has a style, but what is it?

We French set great store by style. To appreciate a man's style we need to know the class to which he aspires. As Jean-Michel puts it, "What would do for a pirate would not do for a pimp." We have both here but Alan is neither because he does not frequent the casino and he wears no scent. He and his wife are known at La Caravelle and La Fringale, but the less reputable places do not know them.

As for his class, I cannot ask him, but in the correspondence I can ask you. *Le patron* says he is a journalist. That would be OK, but we would like it very much more if he were a detective. Of course, if he were a detective he would be at Marseille. Here the secrets are small potatoes. When you answer you will tell me what he is? Meanwhile I am going to keep an eye on him.

I talk with him in the mornings and hear the concerns of his heart. He mentions his dismay at not having work he must do, of being "on liberty," as he puts it. Is he anxious for his income or is he making up a new life? What did he do before?

Why is he so curious about the War here? He questions the old ones about the Resistance and the *maquis*. Nobody talks about those things now in conversation. He will engage one of the old ones in conversation about the past and then ask about the Vichy years. It is very disconcerting to them. There were few heroes of the Resistance here. His questions put people on edge.

That is a peculiar worry of his, like his worry about work. He tells me that it is a comfort to share a worry. "Just giving it voice moves it away from the throat," he says.

I have told Alan my worry that Jean-Michel may send me away because now that his children are grown enough to be out on their own for a few hours at a time, he and his wife have moments of tenderness again and they are embarrassed to have me about at such moments. This is understandable—she has a way that is beautiful, and a most delicious smell—but what am I to do? Sometimes his wife refers to me as the companion of his youth and leaves a hint. I worry about what will become of me. This is the worst thing that I have ever experienced. What is your worst experience?

Dogs understand each other the world over. It is not the same for people. Even if they share a language they do not share their feelings easily, or their worries. Alan and Jean-Michel do not even share a language.

Jean-Michel speaks no English and Alan's French is poor. But they manage. *Le patron* is intrigued. He likes his interviews with Alan, just as he likes the visits from the reporter of *Livre Bleu*. It is pleasant to be asked about your work and adventures by someone who makes notes as you speak. It helps one recognize his own importance. Which proves the homily our Priest gives before the Collection, "It is more blessed to give than to receive."

Allez! Here come the kids.

Regards,
Rodeo

May 5, Hatfield

Monsieur Rodeo—

Most excellent to make a new friend! I bow and stand with dignity to allow the sniffs of introduction, though usually in the sudden presence of a dog your size I growl and stand tall to make sure he keeps a respectful distance. Small dogs like small men must first give the impression of ferocity or all is lost. I got that from your Napoleon—size is style.

I live above my size by projecting fierceness and a reckless unconcern about what may happen. This leads some to think I'm mad, so they're cautious. If you're a small dog or a gambler you can't think about the odds—do so and you lose your nerve. You learn to come on to yourself as The Conquerer. My coming on as a feist dog is no act but it's all theater.

It's good that you're watching out for my master. He is, as you say, my child, although in his eyes I'm the vulnerable one needing protection. I get upset when he goes away. First I get angry and turn over the garbage, then I'm sad for days and shit on the bathmats. I can't help it, I'm angry that he'd risk going out into the world without me. I know how much he misses, what he doesn't see, what he doesn't hear. And, well, I miss him. What else is there? You ask about my worry: my worry is for him, even though he is out of sight. I miss his smell, the sounds of his living, the excitement about him. It is hollow here when he is gone, as if all the furniture had been moved out.

I put in his way when I found it in Zora, the book van, Konrad Lorenz' *King Solomon's Ring*, which tells how we came to live together, wolf and man. Perhaps you know this book? As book-dealing is our business I know such things just as you know about ships and the ways of the sea. I am an autodidact dog.

That poet you mention who thinks dogs have no conversation, no way to express their feelings—where does he think the first poet learned his poetry? I say, suspect anyone who has forgotten how his forebears exchanged news before there were words—the scents, the signs of yawning, smiling and wrinkling the brow. The question is not "Can we speak?" but "Can you hear?" For all animals conversation is a chief joy of life along with lovemaking and eating.

Dogs don't laugh? Aristotle says this? Foolish man. He didn't live with a dog. If he had he would have observed his own dog laughing at his pomposity—not unkindly, just the canine chuckle at the human condition which at one and the same time is so presuming and so pitiful.

Men have forgotten how to stare as closely as we do. We dogs talk through small signs. Men used to watch for these, but when they learned to read their study of little marks replaced the study of small gestures, so they can no longer make out what we say. They are taught to read but they are no longer taught to see.

What did they gain when they lost their delicacy of smell? I know Alan's moods before he does by the scent he gives—the scents of fear or irritation or anger. Their refinement has cost them awareness of that language of each other and the pleasures to be had in stinks and thoroughly ripe meat. I roll in exquisite things whenever I can, and they are disgusted, rush to bathe me, which is a shame. In

my rollings-about I make myself delicious. Their baths leave me uninteresting to those I would entice, and bland and itchy to myself. My smell is my personality, my hat, my shades, my umbrella, my recent glorious past. It takes days of hunting and some good luck to build it up. Your saltwater regimen sounds OK.

In tone, too, much is said. They no longer listen as exactly as we do, but at least in exchange for that they have music. Bach I like, and reggae. Do you like music?

You ask about my training. I'm a philosopher. Philosophers are self-taught. I think deeply, I listen to the conversations at the book van, especially to Tom, who is Alan's partner in that business. I take in TV and Public Radio when I can. I haven't worked out a system like Kant or Nietzsche, but I observe life. I am, to tell it frankly and without boasting, a polymath. Except for math. I haven't perfected my skill with numbers. I'm no card player and I don't like puzzles.

I'm given to maxims. Whenever I come upon something on the van that seems true, some passage or something I hear, I take it up. My friends refer to me as the Maximum dog. My maxim for today is, "Malice invigorates."

I don't know any guide-dog poodles, but I would snap

at the vulnerables of the cur who passed on that canard about one of us leading a blind man into the harbor. As a breed, though, it's true that we are too creative, too full of fun and adventure to work in harness. Our service is pleasure, hilarity and insight. What breed has more spirit, more *brio*?

The business of our names is complicated. "Jefe" is a Spanish word. As the Spanish do not pronounce *j* the sound of my name is "Hefé!"

I'm Jefe to the world, but to Alan's son Benjamin I'm "Little Bear," to his daughter Abigail I am this, to his wife Martha I am that, and Alan has as many names for me as there are minutes in the day. In the end it is only the tone that matters. Words of love are words of love no matter what the words are.

The name I'm proudest of is "Dog of the World." Alan's partner Tom calls me that. He's 85—my age in dog years. Tom and I understand each other. Alan learned most of what he knows about books from Tom, and something of life too. Strange that the truths of life our masters learn from the old ones of their acquaintance are things we dogs knew all along.

There is a story about how I got my name. When I first came into the family Benjamin called me Spike. About that time Alan got a promotion in his company. He became the deputy to the chairman, but his friends joked that he was really in charge of everything and would give them all fat raises. They took to calling him *El Jefe*, which is Spanish for the chief. Alan came home and told the family. They laughed, I barked, the name became mine.

From your letter I can picture you exactly. For my part, I am a tough, low-down black rectangle, twice the size of a swelled-up cat. There's no fat on me and minimal fur as I am kept clipped close with no ornaments. I'm mainly black, but from my mother—Chocolate Momma—I inherited a saddle of dark chocolate.

When I'm standing my nose reaches Alan's knee. I can jump to his waist. I'm a sprinter, and I can turn on a dime. I can catch anything. My best escape is my ability to dodge like the best of our quarterbacks, but there is little I run from. They call my walk a strut. I have large brown eyes which Alan's wife, Martha, says are beautiful, fine sharp teeth and a pointed muzzle. To my embarrassment my ears are a little short and sometimes get stuck on the top of my head. This impairs my dignity. Martha's father jokes that I need ear weights.

You ask about the cat who hurt my knee. It pains me to remember. Alan's daughter Abby went off to college. She was lonely. A roommate found a kitten. It was rude and untrained, a compulsive climber. It climbed the curtains, it climbed trees and howled for help to come down. The firemen came once. The next time the dispatcher asked, "How many times have you seen a dead cat under a tree?"

It was Christmas break. Who'd take the cat? Only Abby. They set out in her car. The cat was not accustomed to the car. Many stops were required. They arrived home late and cranky. The cat was released in the hall. No one had told me to expect a cat! I gave chase. The cat leaped up on the mantel and smashed the ornaments. I was blamed.

Abby took the cat to her room. I kept guard. I sniffed under the door and got my nose clawed. I planned my revenge. The door opened. The cat peered out. I jumped, she swelled. She rose like a bat. She was an aerial cat. She sailed to the ledge on the landing, the special place for the geraniums and the parade of Christmas People. Torn geraniums and fragments of porcelain rained down. I hit the stairs, slipped in the wreckage, and my knee went out. It required an operation. I walk with a limp. I got in one good bite. She's now a bobtail cat.

Dr. Hansen did my operation. I was bandaged and could not walk for a week and then for a month I had stiffness and pain, but now I am without pain for all that I have a slight limp. My limp has its utility: girls and young women offer me sympathy and tender caresses, while foolish dogs misjudge my strength. I take advantage of both. Alan has a bad joint in his hip. He says that when it comes time to have it operated he is going to Dr. Hansen and then he will walk with a limp that gives no pain but attracts women and misleads enemies.

I work on the book van. Alan and I are always collecting books. Bookselling is his work now since his company got sold out from under him. During the winter we organize and price, then weekends from May through October we're in business with Tom selling them. We set up tables beside the small roads. The longer runs we do alone. Tom won't come along on those because we camp out. Alan loves the minimals of camping—bathing in a stream or pond, building fires, the smell of smoke—but Tom doesn't and I don't either. Camp food is irregular, my coat takes on a smoky smell, and I have to keep watch. Sometimes a raccoon is pesky and must be barked off. Once there was a raccoon that turned out to be a skunk and earned me a disgrace. We never set up that week-end.

Just as riding in *Zodiac* can get rough for you, so riding in the book van has its perils. I ride on the front seat next to Alan. Sometimes he piles the books too high, and on a tight turn or a sudden stop a box will come sliding into my place or loose books scatter. Once the *ABC of Reading* came flying up from behind and gave me a bruise.

There's not a lot of money in our business, but Alan likes the people we meet. He does it to meet people and to get their stories. Tom tells us the stories in our books and the stories of their authors. He holds with Addison in *The Spectator*, "I have observed that a Reader seldom peruses a Book with Pleasure 'till he knows whether the writer of it bee a black or Fair Man . . ." Tom can tell you every author black or Fair from Chaucer to Joyce, but mainly he does Shakespeare. He used to be an actor. He likes to hold up a Shakespeare upside down and do the parts from memory. He always gets an applause for that. He likes applause.

Sometimes Tom makes us take our pay in books. Last time out he told the story of the man who sold his shadow for a purse that never empties—*The Wonderful History of Peter Schlemihl*, so we had to take that one home. Then he gave us the poem by X.J. Kennedy about the goose who laid the golden egg, asphyxiated when she poked her head up her fundament to discover the source of her miracle. Such is a day with Tom.

Our book days are busy days from dawn to dusk with the pretty young ones in their skimpy clothes requiring attentions and the older ones offering theirs. I'm given bits of chicken to keep going, Alan makes do with a can of sardines and dips of banana in the jar of instant coffee powder. Our business motto is from Cyrano: "It is good for a man to do some things to excess."

Last time out a skinny kid came up and studied our titles carefully. It was a hot day. He was barefoot but he wore a knit wool cap. His T-shirt was droopy and his pants the same with many pockets that all seemed to be pulling him down. Except for the cap his clothes appeared to be hand-me-downs from someone larger. He had large brown eyes and the scraggy start of a dark red beard. His skin was pale tan.

Alan asked him what he liked to read.

"The Bible," he said, "Everything about the Bible. Books on the past. Ancient people. How we got to where we are."

It was a Sunday morning. Alan mentioned hymn singing, how the best hymn singing he'd ever heard was in Jamaica when he worked there.

"I feel a pulling there," the boy said. "I want to study with the Rastas."

They were off. Alan remarked that the boy's cap had the Rasta colors. The lad said that's why he wore it. They introduced. His name was Dave. He was from New Bedford, an old whaling town to the north of us.

"And your people are from Cape Verde?"

Alan had guessed from his color and where he was born what his people were. Portuguese sailors and escaped slaves settled there a long time ago and bred to these beautiful people. I think there are as many breeds of people as dogs.

Dave poked around for a while. On Alan's urging and after some reading aloud by Tom he went off with a Gibbon for the past and *Brave New World* for the future.

Then we got the Higher Consciousness lady who was up for channeling—getting in touch with who she was before she was born. She had a twenty-five dollar session scheduled to link up with Elijah who would take her back to 1400. In this life she's a librarian and she reads palms. She read Alan's. She said he has two loves, worries a lot, and because he kept his fingers tight together while she read his palm he's pretty tight with money. She bought our $4 *Travels in Arabia Deserta*.

The next visitor bought a fifty cent mystery and pronounced ours "an interesting collection for the side of the road." It came to a sixty-dollar day and so proved the Scotch maxim, "Many a mickle makes a muckle."

Alan's class? We have class in America but it's low class to speak of it. They work out each other's class the way we sniff each other's parts—to pick up where you've been, what you've had, how the sex was there. In the same way that we nose around the privates—he being sniffed standing a little uneasily—they'll ask each other, "What is your job?" and " Where do you live?" If they're upper class they'll ask, "Do you have a home in the country?" and "Where do you go in the winter?" The ones on the make proclaim their class by putting a school sticker on the back of their car.

Dogs are more direct. When I was a puppy and Max up the street wanted to know, I asked Alan, "How much do we have?" "Enough," he answered, "and no debt," which didn't reveal very much to me, but when I told Max he said, "No debt? My God, you are the richest ones around!" So there it is. Do you have debt?

We have a used car and the van that Martha, who is a painter, uses to carry her paintings and Alan uses as the book truck. When it is time to go on the road with his books, Alan tapes signs on its sides and back: "Zora's Good Used Books." Zora is in the Bible. Her name is on the truck when it is the book van because a great-aunt in Missouri was named Zora and she was the first in the family to keep a store. When she started doing that she disgraced the family because storekeeping was for the class below them. They were farmers. But Zora laughed and said she liked the way conversation and cash came together in a store and it sure was cleaner than farming.

We live in a small house with a made-over barn out back that has Martha's painting studio and Alan's work room with the books. Below the barn there's a meander that's become a marsh where a green heron lives and makes his strange calls of love. Then there's a long narrow field for apples, grapes and asparagus. Out beyond the field it gets wild and swampy. A bear lives in there. He's quiet except in the early spring when he first wakes up and is hungry. Then he comes up and takes anything fresh from the mulch pile and pulls down the bird feeder for the sunflower seeds. When he visits we stay inside.

In late winter Alan and I manure the orchard. He gathers barrow-loads of fruit-of-the-horse and I roll in it. It's good for my coat and works into a fine cologne. The horses who create it wonder what the fuss is about and view our gathering with some curiosity. As the way through their paddock is narrow, their curiosity sometimes gets in our way.

The horses are named Spooker and Aramis. In the summer we hear them snort and blow, even at night, to cool off or to blow out a tickle, I don't know. Spooker will tell you right off how she ran for purse money, which makes Aramis impatient. He never won any. They bicker and nip at each other a lot, but when they break out of their paddock for a blissful night of fresh grass and any apples they can find on our trees they stick close together like an old married couple, which proves the adage, There's no bond like contempt. Adages are boned wisdom for weak teeth.

The horses share their barn with the Muscovy ducks we call "the ladies." The ladies are plump and slow. For my exercise I chase them. A rooster lives a few doors down and is very regular in his work with the hens and keeping us on time. He crows before the sun comes up and before it goes down. I like his song.

The mornings now are sweet with the rye in bloom, lilacs, fruit trees. At noon there is the fragrance of new-turned soil as the young boys in baseball hats run their tractors. Until the light is almost gone they go up and down the fields. Their tractors make a purring sound you can hear all around the valley. When a tractor breaks down the boy aboard can usually fix it.

Every older house has its barn for potatoes or tobacco. Even when it's empty you can tell which is the tobacco barn by the smell of curing leaves. They call that smell "tobacco damp." Alan used to smoke, so he sniffs those old barns with hunger when we pass. Sometimes it's a mistake to sniff too deeply before you know what you're sniffing: a potato shed with a few rotten potatoes can knock you over.

All the houses face the road and all the lots run back to the river. When a child marries, a slice is cut off from the whole, road to river. When a child of that child marries a slice comes off the slice, so as the family grows the lots get narrower and narrower. Our piece was a bride's gift to the old lady we bought it from. It's only 60' wide but it runs for two acres to the river and it was rich enough to support her family of five on tobacco and potatoes for ninety years.

My favorite walking place is along the river. I go off leash there and get the news, hunt muskrats and sniff the coyote scat. From what I can tell coyotes eat insects, field mice and rabbits. I guess they cannot catch the muskrats. The muskrats take their picnics of mussels on the bank, but they dive off when I approach. I've never seen a coyote but I can tell you I've been within minutes of surprising one. It's good, life along the river. There's always motion and smells. Do you know *The Wind in the Willows*? That's a fine book about river life. No dog figures in it, but even so it's Alan's favorite book.

Max the husky lives up the street. He barks when I approach his yard on my duties, then crouches in the tall grass and slithers toward us. That's his snake act. He thinks he's sneaking up but his curled tail gives him away. I catch him and he joins us. A little farther along and we pick up Ike. Ike's a black-and-amber setter. His brains got scrambled when he was hit by a car. Now he walks sideways like a crab. He's slightly afraid of me, so I like his company. We like best those friends we have some power over. Which helps explain why men keep dogs and dogs keep men.

Three doors down there's a new Lab in training named Guiness. She's polite on leash but there's mischief in her eye. I like bitches who are looking for trouble.

Smoky and Buddy are near neighbors too, but they're not my particular friends. Buddy is a nearly-blind, stiff-necked old poodle, primped, preened and prissy, who gets all jumpy if you so much as nose his black ass, so to hell with him. Once a week he comes home from The Dog Wash and parades along our fence showing off the blue ribbon in his top knot. He looks like a birthday present or something you'd hang in a tree at Halloween.

Smoky is a portly collie-lab, black and white, fancy in his markings and quite puffed-up about it. He's never on leash. They think he's intelligent because he hasn't walked into the street, but I've never found any conversation in him. He shits in my yard and goes in and out of his house all day because they are smokers and they leave the door open. Smoky smells smoky. One whiff of him knocks out my nose for hours. When we met I told him the joke about legs: The bottom is at the top. He didn't get it.

Alan's work? He was a lawyer until his company got sold; now he's a consultant. He talks on the telephone and writes letters to the people he used to work with. They like him and they need what he remembers because the young ones on the make have no sense of the past. They send him money for his telling them how things got to be the way they are and who has the secrets. Sometimes he has to tell them the secrets. They've about got all his secrets, so what his real work is now he doesn't know. He's looking for it.

Martha is in France to paint. She got a Foundation grant to do it, so she has her work. Alan is unplugged. He doesn't know anyone there. He has no setting. Every man requires a setting, the company of others who know and love him or at least tolerate him. That's why Americans love their jobs and Frenchmen love their villages.

At first Alan spent his time wandering around your town. He found the idea of doing anything or nothing hard to wake up to. He depends on the daily Next Next Next like coffee. Is this longing for work a uniquely American dilemma? Is it in the national genes? The men of our acquaintance are all conscious of their immigrant forebears and how frantic they were to make a landing and claw out some beachhead of security.

It probably takes ten generations of being in one place to feel secure that there's enough. It's the place that gives that feeling of security, not the size of the account. I listen to Alan's friends talk and I realize that for most of them there will never be enough. They're afraid that without more they'll die on the way to high ground. Work is their place; the money they get is their proof of life, or, as Alan's friend Barry puts it, "What they pay you is how much they love you."

Ben tells me that in France people retire with nice pensions and return to their villages, to their place there, their table for the morning coffee. They admire their bodies and dress with care.

When Americans finish their years of work, where can they go? What has become of their village? All their lives they've been moving, but they've rarely gone home. The village they remember from childhood has been abandoned or built over. Their parents have left, the home place has been sold. Nothing stays the same.

America is not a country for the past—it's all today and tomorrow. Instead of a place to hold on to and be held by, there's money. As for pensions, they're pretty scant, and anyway the takeover pirates raid them when they can. Our friends don't save. Everything they get they spend, and the few who do save worry about paying for their health. There's no national insurance here. That would be "Socialism," a thing which makes our Republicans go amok, so I wonder what sort of republic they picture.

Alan's interest in the War must have to do with his living now where it happened. During the War a refugee came to live in his home in Maryland. He said she looked like a ghost. She was rescued in your part of France.

It sounds very good for you, your sailing work with the children, but I wouldn't like it. I'm more an inside dog with the books. I spend a lot of time thinking with my eyes closed. As for children, I like them well enough in general but not in the specific. I like watching in the morning when the school bus proceeds down our street. Every few houses it stops and the waving mothers and the tail-wagging dogs put their little ones aboard. Then the dejected dogs and relieved mothers walk back to their kitchens. That's the best time to observe our town dogs.

I dislike small children. I like them even less than cats. The worst are the little ones that stumble into me and pull my ears. When we have the book van set up children chase me. Because I'm their size or smaller they presume to play with me like a football. They take liberties. They step on my paws. They pretend that I'm a pony. It's different with you—you're of a size and shape that makes them wary. I bet they don't stumble into you and gurgle as they pull your ears. They do this to me because they think I'm cute and harmless.

My practice with children who rush up is the same as with any dog that presumes: I snarl and show my teeth. That dispels the illusion of cuteness. No waiting to see how the encounter will turn out; my rule is, Growl first! If that doesn't work I back off snarling, and if they chase me I give the bite. I always aim for the lowest parts and then the underside of the throat.

I particularly dislike Colleen next door. She's eight, fat, and on the road to trouble. She comes around when nobody's home and pretends to be the Mailman. She bangs on the door and yells in a false voice, "Gas Man." She rings the doorbell. She slams the door knocker. She awakens me. My heart starts pounding! I rush downstairs in disarray. The Gas Man! An intruder! I go crazy at the door. Then I hear her giggle. The thing is, her parents both work, so she comes home, there's no one around, I'm the only company she's got. It would be a dull world without enemies.

Enemies: The other day a neighbor's hound named Caesar came bounding up full of piss and presumption. I've warned him before, I warned him again, but on he charged. I got in some pretty good bites before I let Ben pull me off. Caesar ended up whimpering in his master's arms and calling me a "nasty ass dog!" "Right on, man!" I yelled back. The cur just moaned. I was so pleased I did my prizefighter swagger all the way home. I may be small but I've got *attitude*! For all they tut-tut my toughness act, Ben and Alan like my attitude. They're small too.

The day after I met up with Caesar I told Max about it. He knows Caesar. Caesar gave him a run and some nips a while back. Max likes the "nasty ass" monicker. He said it's my reckless passion that's terrifying. Reckless passion sounds like something out of the soaps we watch. Do you watch the soaps?

You mention your concern about being in the way at moments of tenderness. Try this: When the time of tenderness comes, ask to be let outside, even if it is raining. Do so out of politeness and discretion. Make it a rule to give them their privacy. Don't betray the slightest jealousy or reluctance. Bound to the door with joy and lightness in your step. Jean-Michel will be grateful.

The important thing is to act. That way you'll avoid depression from feeling in the way. At the same time, the more indifference you show, the more Jean-Michel will value you. You will find this in Benjamin Franklin, who probably got it from Montaigne.

By the way, are there dogs in Montaigne? No dogs in Franklin, which makes me think he was a pretty cold fish. He had many assignations but no passions, so he can write about affairs of the heart with coolness. Your Montaigne was probably the same way. He said, "I don't know whether I play with my cat or she plays with me," so I think he was pretty much a cat himself. No one would write that about his dog.

When Alan is here I sleep in his bed. Do you sleep in Jean-Michel's? Martha doesn't like it, especially when I'm wearing a rich cologne, but even then Alan will bury his nose in my belly fur. He likes the smell of dog—not the outer layer of goose ordure and rot and the dead meat that I've rolled in and the residue of pond juice from my pursuing the ladies, but my sweet silky underneath fur which is always clean and keeps me warm.

Do you get fleas? It's flea season with us. They're a torment. I spend hours cleaning and preening and rolling in dust but I can't beat them. Max recommends tearing open an ant hill and letting the ants clear them out. Doesn't work for me. When the fleas are bad I'll submit to a bath. I'm not allowed in the bed when there are fleas. It's not my fault. They lurk in the grass.

I've heard of Rodeo. I asked Ben about Rodeo's film, but he doesn't follow Westerns. He prefers your French films like *400 Blows*, which I found very sad. If only that little boy had had a dog! By the way, have you seen *My Life As a Dog?* A young boy worries about the dog sent up in Sputnick. I've wondered about him too. I guess he's still out there. Have you rented *Titanic* yet? It's funny for the rats running up the hallway in that brand-new ship. They have their own scene. It's almost as good as the end of *The Odyssey* when Odysseus comes home after his long voyage and only his dog recognizes him. What was the name of that dog?

I admire your literature. Here is my favorite line in La Fontaine's *Fables*: *"Deux coqs vivaient en paix; une poule survint."* Send me something that you admire.

I hear Ben at the door! It is time for Leash!

Regards to Rodeo from his new friend—

Jefe

May 25, Cassis

Dear Ben,

A month in and we've settled our work routines, figured out how the apartment works, where to find things in town, the hours of *La Poste*. Martha's located some *paysages*, I've got my laptop set up. I blew the printer the day we arrived. My $5 Chinese converter exploded and the lights went out.

M'sieur Ducroux, our landlord, had to come over and show me in the closet the green button you push to reset the fuse. He offered to help me find a new converter, so we went in his car and visited all the *bricoleurs* in Marseille. No luck. We settled for an *apéritif* on the port. After a while it didn't matter that no one had what I needed, I had made a new friend. Anyway I think the printer's dead; it gave off a bad smell when the lights went out.

So every afternoon now before she closes I carry my computer to Annie at Buroprim to have my day's work printed. Annie's afraid of *Le Virus*. She's convinced that it's transported on the disk, so she won't allow me to bring mine in for printing. She has to slip her own disk into my *ordinateur* to make the transfer. Then she prints it.

As she goes through her operations at the computer she sings gypsy songs. She has a sweet voice. She is not young. Her hair is long and thin and startlingly black. She is a deep-sea fisherman. The Buroprim office is filled with photographs of her standing beside the huge fish she's killed on holiday in Madagascar.

She has large dark eyes and wears gleaming copper hoops in her ears. She has lunch with a friend every day on the port. They drink a lot of wine with their *salades* and sardines. I used to wait for her to return from lunch at 3 P.M.—which is the time the sign on her door says the office will reopen—but she was often late and usually too looping then to perform the tricky operations the computer requires. She's clearer at six so I go back at six.

Because paper is expensive I've asked Annie to print my stuff on scrap. The other side is a quiz from a grade-school math primer, junked because the pages got misnumbered. I begged her to save the lot and print my work on it. She wasn't happy about this, not because she wants to sell fresh paper—she says she makes nothing on the paper—but because "Recycling is not a proper thing to do with a letter that one delivers to *La Poste*!"

Concerning recycling, I just saw Marie Laurent, the bent-legged old fishmonger, haul her morning's load of entrails to the water's edge and chuck them in bit by bit to the yelling gulls. She and the gulls have a talk together. She could put that stuff in a can for the town truck, but she likes her visits with the gulls. She sets up early every morning in the same gray-blue dress and gets well-bloodied and fishy at her work. She waves to her friends as they go by. She has a wonderful smile.

We couldn't do this stint if you weren't there to take care of Jefe, the mail, the house. I hope you're getting in some good writing time. For our part we're struggling to "Milk it dry!" as Tom urges on his postcards.

Since all our mail comes to our landlord's box, he reads the postcards. He is courteous and formal. He used to teach English in Marseille. His speech is that of a genteel pre-War Englishman.

The other day he knocked with our mail.

"Alan, I regret to intrude, but my intrusion is compelled by this "Milk it dry!" message you are receiving. To what does this milking refer?

Tom switched his message. "Keep your traction!" will bring the Monsieur back to our door pretty soon.

Noon. 80° on our porch. Up and out early this morning to go painting with Martha at Presqu' île before the sun gets too high. The sun's so bright that even in full shade it sucks the figures off my computer screen. To get the most shade I work in a pine grove where there are a lot of mourning doves. All day long they sing an endless three-beat coo-coo—coo, coo-coo—coo. How they stand it I can't imagine. They don't do anything but flutter and sing. A lady feeds them from her porch. She clanks the trays when she puts out their food and gets a cloud of doves. She's probably a *fonctionnaire,* pigeon-feeding on a government grant. Sometimes I hear shooting nearby. Wild birds are eaten here.

I like living on the coast. The sea is noisy and alive, banging and heaving, changing color, fragrant. Our town is an old fishing port. At 4 A.M. the boats go out. They're small, 21' long, 7 wide, built here to a design any waterman at any time would understand and approve. Each has a little glassed-in shack to one side at the stern. These boats are bravely painted and run on single-lung diesels, wonderful sturdy little engines, simple and slow. With fuel enough they could make Gibraltar. During the War some did.

Each boat carries three or four tattered flags on poles to mark the buoys along the fisherman's net lines. For luck the flags are torn from old shirts and underwear. Some are black, most are red, one looks like it was torn from an orange plaid shirt. Coming in, the boats look very gay carrying their flutters and followed by the cloud of gulls that breakfasts on what gets tossed as the nets are picked.

Fish was the mainstay and the town was tiny until they built the casino. Now there are 5,000 residents. The people you see on the port divide between those who visit the casino and those who don't. One look and you know—the shoes, the gold chain, the hands. Gamblers have delicate hands. Must come from counting. And they wear strong scent, florals to mask the musk of fear.

The thrill of gambling is the fear in it, but you don't want anyone to notice, so the wise gamblers anoint themselves with Floris and make every effort to sniff out their opponents' hands. Some bring their dogs to help, especially the gypsy ladies who keep their small poodles and Yorkies in baskets on the gaming tables. Few realize what those ladies are up to.

I went and watched the dogs. The dogs watched the other players and the ladies modestly watched their dogs. Now and then a dog would give his mistress a look. They could count, those dogs! They knew their cards and could keep a hand in mind. Those who hold that dogs can't talk should button their pockets with the care they guard their flies.

The dominant physical feature on this coast is a rock formation called the Cap Canaille. From our porch it looks like a red bulldog lying on his belly. Behind us there are limestone mountains scraped clean by glaciers and burned off so many times they look snow-capped. The stone is easily worked. The port is walled and paved with blocks of it. Some pieces are cut for sinks.

Overlooking the port there's a medieval castle which is illuminated from below at night. Of a similar castle on Cyprus, Rose Macaulay remarked to Lawrence Durrell, "Have you ever wondered how it is that the utilitarian objects of one period become objects of aesthetic value to succeeding ones? This thing was constructed purely to keep armies at bay, to shatter men and horses, to guard a pass. . . . Does time itself confer something on relics and ruins which isn't inherent in the design of the builder?"

The shops and flats facing the water are beige, yellow, tan, a faded blue. The shutters are chalky purple, pale green, rouge. Behind the port there are weavings of alleys and steep narrow streets. When a car comes, pedestrians and dogs flatten against the buildings or slip into doorways. Overhead the day's washing flutters from spindly wire racks hung out the windows. The local soap has a heavy fragrance. If the breeze is right you can smell a wash long before you see it.

There is a town beach with a picnic patio. In the afternoons the skateboarders come to exhibit their jumps, a dozen boys aged 12 to 16 in pants too large. A slightly younger company of girls occupies the benches and applauds the most daring successes, which involve working up a great speed on the flat, soaring up the steps, winding among the benches and sailing back down. One purple-shirted boy has mastered this ballet. At the end of his performance he exchanges kisses with his audience in the polite French "buss buss" way.

One afternoon a lovely budding pigtailed girl in shorts and T-shirt arrived with a board. I'd never

seen a girl skateboarder there before. The boys stopped their dance so she could exchange the usual kisses with them. The audience of girls she ignored. Purple Shirt put on his best display as she demurely circled and did a few easy jumps to the lowest step. Purple Shirt danced for his Queen. He must have got the steps right because they left together.

When I finish at Annie's I go over to Le Bar du XXième Siècle for a beer. The regulars' dogs stand with them at the bar or sit under their tables. They lie down but they do not sleep. Even with their eyes closed the dogs in the bar are on alert.

No one is hurried. A table of old men play cards for money in the back watched over by two or three kibitzers. Out front a lady sits nursing her beer. She's there when I arrive, she's there when I leave. I catch her eye and we nod. Her hair was flaxen once. She is lean with bright blue eyes.

The patron of the XXième is a large man tending to fat. The round of his head is not large enough for the round of his body. Martha and I went in for coffees the other morning just after he'd opened. With a feather duster he was daintily brushing his bottles one by one. The card games were going, the kibitzers in place, the old lady posted out front. Perhaps she is the *sécurité* ?

Because I'm cut off—no friends in town, few people I can understand—something I just came upon in an Auden poem rings true to me: "And home is miles away, and miles away/No matter who, and I am quite alone/And cannot understand what people say,/But like a dog must guess it by the tone."

Every morning I hear a high excited bark that goes on for hours. The dog starts barking on the port and ends up on the water, sometimes pretty far out with a group of small sailboats.

At first I couldn't find him, he wasn't on the port, he wasn't in any of the cafés. Following the barking, I worked my way around to the lighthouse side, past the marine railway, the shipyard, the chandler's, and the place where they repair boat motors. I came upon a tan shepherd lying down in front of The School of the Sea—Sailing Lessons Offered, FF300 the beginning course. The dog looked up and cocked his head. His ears are tall and black, very delicate.

A swarthy guy in T-shirt and shorts was working inside at his desk. We introduced. His name is Jean-Michel Beaujon. I asked him if I could photograph his dog. He was friendly, told me the dog's name—Rodeo (the dog's head cocked again when he heard his name)—and stroked him while I took a picture. He told the dog to let me pet him too. The phone rang, the man went back inside. I stayed there for a long time petting his dog. I began to talk to him like I talk with Jefe.

Rodeo wasn't eager to be petted. He's a wolf. There was none of this roll-on-my-back-and-scratch-my-belly-stuff, but he was patient with my talking, so I visit him every morning now. Prisoners, patients, and old people should all have dogs to talk to.

Rodeo is serious and dignified. He's totally committed to his master. He won't be distracted while Jean-Michel is moving about, but when things are quiet he's sympathetic in a way that is common with dogs and rare with humans. I talk to him and tell myself things I didn't know.

He tells me about life in the town and life in general. Only Rabelais in all of literature is on to what dogs can tell us. Only Rabelais understands the significance of the sniff.

M'sieur Beaujon is patient as I struggle to make myself understood. He works with handicapped adults so he's used to people who have difficulty making themselves understood. He's also a coach. He runs the sailing school here and teaches little ones how to swim. He does water therapy with handicapped children.

When it is time for school the dog and his master move quickly, Rodeo bounding like a ballerina, every step lifting up, while in one run J-M hustles the gas can, bilge pump and oars to his large rubber *Zodiac* and leaps in, the dog right behind.

I sat through the first class of the new session, 10 girls aged 8 to 11. Jean-Michel greeted each one formally and showed the class how to put on the life vests and collect the masts, centerboards and tillers and place them properly in the boats. The boats were lined up on the wharf. J-M sat in one and with energy and excitement described how to handle the sheet, the tiller, the way of the wind in the sail, the luff, the care necessary in coming about.

Suddenly he grabbed the boom, swung it against his head and pretended to fall overboard. They caught on! All this with total seriousness—his voice at one moment loud and rapid, at another low and almost growling. Sometimes he'd ask a question. Every eye was on him, especially Rodeo's. Rodeo panted the whole time. What if we had teachers like Jean-Michel teaching math to ten-year-olds?

I feel like the boy with the egg—the schoolboy who, to learn the responsibility of being a parent, is given a fresh egg to tend. He must carry it with him at all times. He must keep it warm. He must not drop it! The Mariner dog Rodeo and his master have become my egg.

Martha and I have become regulars at La Caravelle which is at the far end of the port and so is cheaper than the restaurants catering to the gamblers. The gamblers don't like to walk so far, and besides, they want to be seen at the center of things. As for La Caravelle's plates, they're large and the flavors are not too delicate.

Our waitress is a tomboy-tough from Paris, a one-time *gamine* in her imagining. She's quick and jokey and walks with a young boy's bounce. She's pretty in a rough way, her short hair dyed the Marseille mahogany which is the fashion here, something of a good figure still, but she looks like she got into a fight and someone smashed her nose. She could be 40. She's raucous with her friends at the bar up front and laughs a great whooping cackle.

We came in late one evening and heard singing from the kitchen. I asked Robert, *le patron* about it.

"That's Issa. She's a *chanteuse* from Paris. She sings on the stage there and in the cabarets. She's here for her vacation. Perhaps she is an illegal from Oran? Perhaps she has no papers? I don't know her past. She speaks of a house in Algeria and paints for us the picture of her estate with many *hectares* of orange groves, but who knows? Tonight she sings."

Robert yelled and out came our waitress. She gave us a song. The woman who sang to us was not the same person who'd roared with her friends up front and jollied us through our meals. She came to our table and stood there for a moment shaking out her hair and adjusting her body as if she were shaking off the present and going somewhere else. She became someone else. In a husky voice she sang "Je ne regrette rien." My hair went up.

I asked if she had a tape of her singing. Yes, she will get us a tape from Paris. I asked if it were true that she sings in the cabarets in Paris. She raised her eyes and went behind the bar. After some fishing around she came back with a show poster, Issa all right, but different.

"That was before the accident," she said.

I've been asking around about the War here. There's a plaque on the road to Marseille for a *Resistant* aged 22 shot there by the Germans in 1943 (*fusillé* is the word for what happened to him). On the walk to the lighthouse there's another plaque commemorating the Free French sailors and their submarine sunk in the Baie, December, 1943. But evidence? Memory? Nothing stark at first. Then you notice a queer stone box at the end of the Lombard, so darkened now it almost blends with the crumbling rock. A machine gun hut.

The old ones have memories, mainly of hunger. There was the *Résistance*, they say, but there are no forests here, the *maquis* required forests. . . There were reprisals.

Did the yoke lie easy? Were there Jews in Cassis? Protesters? *Maquis*? In the handsome office of *Le Maire* was a list kept like the one in Bordeaux of children and others to be sent away?

Who the hell am I to ask? Asking about a time so murky implies a judgment. I'd cringe if they asked me, "Were you in Vietnam? Did you protest?" And yet, late at night now, at the sound of a small truck grinding up the hill on our port road, what do the old ones hear?

A hint of the old tensions is the reference on the plaque near the lighthouse that the submarine was one of *La France Libre*—not part of the French fleet. By the terms of Vichy the fleet was to stay out of the fight. Being close to the large fleet port at Toulon, Cassis was a fleet town, conservative, suspicious of the Free French. And perhaps Vichy was not so bad?

I've heard a story that submarines would slip into the deep cuts here to supply the *maquis* and take off refugees. I want to find out where this happened. I wonder if there's any record of who they picked up. During the War a girl came to live with us in Maryland, a distant relation whose family had protested the Nazis. She and her family were jailed. She had escaped. A submarine picked her up.

Jefe would like it here. Swagger and strut are the norm, dogs wander into the stores for treats and go with their people to the cafés. Few are on leash. The French do not dock their poodles' tails and all the males have kept their balls.

A hug for you and the Jefe dog—

Love, Dad

June 1, Hatfield

Dear Mom and Dad—

Things OK here, quiet except for the Deeres rumbling up and down the road. Most everything is planted, the new corn is nosing up, teams of black men are bent over tucking in rows of tiny tobaccos. Apples and pears are set. We've had a lot of asparagus. I'm sick of asparagus.

They must be counting on a big tobacco crop. Every t-barn for miles is getting a new roof or some siding replaced. Even a couple of the falling-down ones are getting revived. All the farmers are praying that the frost is past; Chaz the barber tells me that one touch of frost and the crop is lost.

Jefe was pretty gloomy for a while after you left, but now after dinner we take long walks on the Smith campus and he runs into some dog friends. Amazing what a dog chat does for his cheerfulness. I tried to take him jogging but he'd peter out five doors down where the two Labs live. So we go out on the bike together. He loves bike rides, sits in the basket and claims to know every dog we pass. It's a curious thing about dogs, they don't ignore each other. They may be strangers, but they have news for each other. I ring the bell and Jefe barks.

This morning, though, he's pissed. I went down to New York for the night, put down the puppy papers, set out his food. He did things on your rug upstairs and didn't eat. Not much better a couple of weeks ago when I went down for two nights and had Pamper-A-Pet come over Saturday and Sunday. He sure can mope.

Last week I did the Heimlich maneuver on a dog. Yvonne next door was tossing tennis balls to Smoky. She'd waddle, he'd waddle, a low pitch, he'd lurch up and usually miss. But then he caught one dead on and it jammed in his mouth. He couldn't breathe.

He was flopping around and fading like a hooked fish. I tried to pry it out, no go. So I rolled him over and whomped him on the diaphragm. The ball exploded out.

Smoky is sore and sore at me. Jefe watched all this with some satisfaction. Smoky would never let him near that tennis ball.

Haven't made it up to Vermont, haven't talked to Tom. I write, read, run, eat, walk, write, read, eat, bicycle and sleep. Some TV, some videos. *Blue Velvet* and *The Longest Day,* those Pagnols you like. One for you, *A Self-Made Hero*—French.

Thanks for the poems. De la Mare is new to me. I'm reading a lot of Wilde, a bio of Nabokov, some Paul Auster, and Julien Barnes's *Flaubert's Parrot*. Wilde's the best, the gay playing straight, the radical playing regular, a Mick in the bargain and in what clothes! Amazing that he pulled it off as long as he did. Wonder if R.L.S. knew him. Who and what didn't he take on? Who's like Wilde today?

Dreary, the daily Clinton stories. They've got him tied down and every day take another bite. But they won't kill him. He's worth more to them bleeding shame and embarrassment.

Best! Best! for the painting. Keep up the notes and postcards. Glad you've got a local dog but don't forget your Main Man.

Let up on the War stuff, Dad. It wasn't your war. You'll never find those people anyway. It could have been anywhere on that coast.

Ben

June 2, Cassis

Jefe my gallant! Boss dog! Maximum!

A quick note as a class of young sailors has graduated and we have the Pentecost holiday. *Le patron* does some work on the boats now. The sails are strong nylon but sometimes they tear. Jean-Michel has a sewing machine in the tackle room. He works it with his feet. The patch he uses is bright pink. He can buy white patch but he likes the color. He is proud to have his mends show on *les voiles*.

"Hefé"—I've got the pronunciation correct? "Little Chief." That would make a good name for a French dog, especially for one of the clever ones of your size who accompany the women to the Casino and tip them off when they should bid and when to fold. They ride in baskets, those Magi, but it does not sound to me like you are the type to ride in a gypsy lady's basket.

So you admire Napoléon! He earned his first glory right here as a junior officer defending this coast. In the confusion of our *Révolution* the English sought to take advantage. They blockaded Toulon.

Napoléon scoured the hill towns for artillery. Ancient

pieces were dragged into place. He commenced a bombardment as if there was no limit to his ammunition. With shot falling like hail all around him, the English admiral turned tail. At that moment Napoléon's battery had shot its last, but who was to know?

That was his making. He was ushered into Paris a hero. One of his cannon was placed here. It is said that he came once to inspect it. He chose a good spot: when the Germans occupied Cassis they mounted a shore gun exactly where Napoléon had placed his. Now the Foundation has an amphitheater there with grass and oleanders and bougainvillaea which are splendid in this season.

It is good that they have made that place so pretty. Sixty years ago it was shrouded in concertena wire and looked out on a scuttled cruiser placed to keep your soldiers out. There was nothing for the dogs to eat then. Even the people starved.

By the way, what is a foundation?

Alan has explained a little his interest in the *Résistance*. A woman he is related to came here by the evasion line—*le réseau d'évasion*—out of Germany. She escaped by floating down the Rhône with a young soldier from this region. A submarine picked her up. So many sought to escape, there must have been something special about her that she was selected for the rescue.

Last week *le patron* and I walked Alan to Port-Miou where the quarry ships used to come in and collect their freights of cut stone. The water is very deep in Port Miou. It is one of the *calanques*. It is the place where the submarines nosed in during the War to make their connections. Alan stared at that place very hard as if to memorize every detail of the staging, the old ironwork, the ladders down. *Le patron* explained about the pirates who had used that place and about the ships of Napoléon's time that had patroled it, but Alan wanted only to hear about the submarines.

I liked the story of your dispatching the presumptuous Caesar, I groaned when I read how you injured your knee. It was glorious, that chase you gave! I can smell the torn geraniums and picture the fine little porcelains flying to their destruction as the cat caroomed. And now, yes! I can taste your good bite! But then, at the ultimate moment to wrench your knee—ah, my friend, I ache for your indignity, for the lost opportunity to give that sneering wretch the *coup de grâce*! I feel a large growl welling in my throat. Did you save the tail as a souvenir?

It is hard for cats here. The whole of Provence is dominated by dogs. I do not dislike cats myself as I have no familiarity with them. But it is in the blood of dogs to rush at cats and send them off, swelled-up the way they get. The birds, too, harass the cats, especially the magpies. They gather like crows and swoop down on any cat they see. So our cats are furtive. There is a circus of cats which is such a novelty that when it comes to the port in the autumn it draws many francs from the pockets of the idlers and the papas whose children rush to see it.

The one cat I do not chase for amusement is Gérard who rides to work on the shoulder of the strange boy Victor who does sanding and painting in the shipyard. This boy is always to be seen wearing his cat. It must be hot, that muff. Victor cannot speak. He points and he is told. His cat Gérard has a curious habit. When it is the season of the *cigales*—our cicadas—he is released from Victor's shoulder and attacks them on the pine trees where they are making their music. He will jump up three or four feet to capture one in his mouth, and then he eats it. The magpies chase him when he does this; perhaps they regard the *cigales* are their *apéritifs*?

Today we have a huge wind, a *rafale* force 8, I am sure. All the flags are taut. There are no small boats on the Baie. The sailing yachts are in the harbor, tight-reefed. The Navy helicopter does not make his survey this morning. Pine needles drive through the air like nails. The dust blows and there are even small stones in the air. Not good! There is no rain, it is hazy, so this is the *sirocco* from North Africa where it is very hot and dry. There are swells and whitecaps. I'm not sure that Alan will swim today. The water is not clear.

Le patron loves this weather. He whistles and yells in the gusts. At the moment he is importuning a yacht owner for the use of his vessel. He loves to sail in this wind. He'll run before it with every inch of sail. We'll fly! We tack, and he whoops like one of your red Indians as the vessel heels, its bones groaning as we come about. We heel so far over we take on water. Jean-Michel is a fine racing sailor but he has no big boat of his own. Too expensive.

It is market day. The Parking is closed for the farmers who come in with their produce and the others with their breads, sausages, honey, bolts of cloth. The vendors put out tables with their goods and large square parasols to shade them. But the *vent*! A large gust came and lifted one of the parasols with its table! Tables and parasols were overturned. There were yells and screams and much barking. The little round cheeses of the goat went spinning. The honey man's soaps bit the dust. Melons and onions, cherries and asparagus rolled about. The lady who sells loose herbs and spices from the open boxes—her stock went up in a cloud!

For us dogs the confusion was wonderful. I ate three of the small round brebis cheeses and a thick wedge of pâté an elderly lady dropped in her alarm.

But in the confusion I took a shard in my left front pad. There is broken glass here as there is everwhere, but this wind has disturbed it, so instead of lying flat the pointed end was aimed up and speared me. I cried out when it happened, more in surprise than in pain. *Le patron* stopped and was very kind. As he dug it out with his knife he told me the story of Androcles and the Lion. I licked his hand in gratitude when he finished the operation. When we passed the boatyard he secured some hot tar and applied it to my wound. This cleans it and protects it from the wear of walking. Now I hobble. *Le patron* says that by the time the tar has worn off my wound shall have healed. The shard was almost the size of a claw.

Mon ami, I hand you my apologies. *Le patron* says I should never have asked about your class, not even in a correspondence! He says America is too new a country for it, too poor in society. Alan has no class. It was a rudeness on my part to mention it. France has had culture and society for 1,000 years. In France a family has to have been established for 200 years before its class can be considered.

Anyway, even if Alan could trace his origins back 200 years—a difficult thing to do in your country I think?— his work as the shopkeeper Zora in his rolling book stall would establish his as something other than a class of distinction. In other words, your family is like ours.

I thought because of his work and manner he might be an eccentric aristocrat. We have them here in some numbers, but they are mostly English. Forgive me if I offended you. It was an act of ignorance on my part. But it is curious, what he does. Who pays him to make notes and photographs?

The strategy of Benjamin Franklin may be working. When the moment of tenderness arrives I now rush smiling to the door and excuse myself. At first Jean-Michel was startled; now he seeks to detain me and pay some attentions. As I wait at the door his wife teases that she wishes to sing to me. She even brings me morsels from the café.

Jean-Michel is almost apologetic about my departures, as if he feels some guilt. Is this also part of the technique Franklin? As he lets me out he gives my ruff a shake and says, "Good man!" as if he were my uncle. All this is new, and he does not ask where I go! At last I have my liberty and it is very sweet, though I tell you it has increased my appetite and I have not seen a film in weeks. Obsidienne and Gigi have enjoyed my favors. I am almost an Independent.

Obsidienne is the woman of my heart. I tell you frankly my friend, I do like being off the leash with her. She is the one I dream of. When I tell *le patron* my feelings for her he laughs and calls me a *roué*. But my feelings for her are very sincere. For the moment Obsidienne and I are in the most delicious part of our acquaintance.

Alan is 58? *Le patron* is younger. He's never told me his age exactly, but he is younger. The French do not give their years so easily, but I'd guess he is about 50. He was born in Algiers, so he is what they call here a "blackfoot," which means he comes from Africa. His feet are not black, but his skin is darker than Alan's. He is what you call swarthy. The silver is beginning at the sides of his head. With us the age shows in the muzzle. Alan says you have some whiteness in your muzzle. You must be a grandfather many times over!

Jean-Michel got into some trouble when he was a boy. He wears tattoos on his arms from that time. One is of a green serpent. He says he was a *petit dans la délinquance*. He stole automobiles. He says of himself, "When I was young I was a thug. I was a Chicago guy from the movies."

He did not go to jail but the reform school he was sent to was almost the same thing. Later, for something more serious he had to serve a term in the French Army—the corps for delinquents. The French Army in North Africa was strict, the duty hard. It was during the Algerian war for independence, the time of the FLN. He saw terrible things in that war, acts of cruelty to children and women and to the helpless ones. He does not talk about it, but when the subject comes up his face tightens in a way that I never observe otherwise.

When he was 20 and just released from the Army he was filled with bitterness. He had no kindness for himself, no kindness for anyone. At that moment he was about to become a true criminal.

Two things changed his life. He learned to command his body through the techniques of Yoga, and he met l'Abbé Simon.

L'Abbé Simon was a high-diver. He made exhibition dives to get money to help children and others injured in that war. He was 73 years old and still diving when Jean-Michel encountered him. The first thing he taught *le patron* was how to manage the high dives.

As *le patron* came to trust him they got on to other things. L'Abbé agreed that the discipline of Yoga was excellent. "Only if you have command of your body can you command your spirit," he said. "But," he added, "you need some work of necessity, some work only you can do to know joy in your life."

He undertook to help Jean-Michel find his work of necessity, but first there was the difficulty of Jean-Michel's record as a delinquent: No one would make a place for a person who had his record with the police. Moreover, like an unrepentant, *le patron* wore the serpent of his gang on his forearm. He would not be allowed to enter France.

Somehow l'Abbé helped him clear his record and correct his papers. Still, Jean-Michel would not disfigure the serpent on his arm. He did not want to forget who he had been. "I was the serpent," he says. "I must remind myself always that I knew evil."

He will talk about his delinquency now, but at 20 his dossier prevented him from getting any employment, any schooling, any social benefit. No one at *La Poste* where the benefits are arranged would meet with him. He was an outcast. He slept in the street.

L'Abbé gave him a home and work aiding the handicapped. *Le patron* decided to follow l'Abbé's example through a way of life that teaches command of the body.

He begins his students with the first lessons of Yoga—the breathing exercises, the movements of the eyes, the head, the Cobra, the stretches, the care in controlling even the smallest movement, the importance of flexing. The virtue of Yoga is the loosening of the spine. One becomes calm then; one can absorb awareness. Late in the Yoga classes he teaches them to "look with soft eyes." Even now *le patron* continues his Yoga studies. You have your philosophy? The Yoga is his.

Then he teaches them to become confident of something they can do with their bodies. A skill. He teaches them how to survive on the water. It may seem strange to you, a breed of water dog, but for them learning to be comfortable in the water involves mastering their greatest fear—drowning.

In our school they learn to swim in rough water and sail in all weathers. *Le patron* believes that if he can teach them to master those things they will have learned the pattern of mastering other things.

The swimming comes quickly enough in most cases. They begin with the flutterboard in shallow water. Then he holds them so they can float on their backs. They scream with pride when they have achieved that! Everything else follows.

Jean-Michel told me what l'Abbé said to him when he became his disciple: " 'There are two doors, the right door and the left.' L'Abbé would pull my ear and smack me—I was a grown man of 20!—when he saw me heading toward the wrong door.

"I would get angry when he pulled my ear. It was painful, but I respected him for his cross and his years, so I did not strike him and go away. I obeyed. I now understand that he taught me how to begin. Who can teach you more than that? Or give you more?"

Jean-Michel has been conducting the sailing school for more than twenty years. I wasn't around at the start, but I have heard the story of how he raised money to buy the boats. He remembered what l'Abbé Simon had done to raise money—the diving.

Le patron asked his friends to help him build a tower near the port. They worked for weeks gathering the lumber and making the construction. Then one day they put up signs announcing that Jean-Michel, at risk to his life, would dive from this tower at Port-Miou on Saturday in the afternoon to raise money for his sailing school. The signs described it as *Le Plongeur De L' Espoir*—The Diver of Hope.

Naturally everyone in town wanted to help this brave man. A *fête* was organized. *Apéritifs* were arranged. La Patisserie Lion said they would furnish cakes to the audience. M'sieur Prévot, the Butcher, promised his famous pâtés. From L'ou Cassidenne came *baguettes* to eat with the pâté. The

Tunisian family that owns La Fringale came with their *pizzas jambon*. M'sieur Sauvat the green-grocer sent his son with a jug of the spicy olives of Provence and the cheeses of the goat that he is known for. Le France and Le Bar de la Marine put out free *boissons*. There was abundance and there was *amitié*. People here still speak of it as a grand *fête*.

Le patron raised what money he needed. More. He wanted to buy ten of the little flat-bottomed boats of the class called "Optimist." He got twelve, plus some extra sails and *Zodiac*, which is his command boat, and the motor for it which makes a great noise and a wonderful smoke. "It proved to me the Parable of Loaves and Fishes," he says.

We do not get a fortune out of our work. It sounds like your book-van venture. We do it for joy and a survival. *Le patron* lives simply. He has a suit for church, but his everyday clothes are T-shirts and bathing shorts, sometimes just a black diving brief. And the telephone. Alan asked him about wearing the telephone. *Le patron* explained that he wears it for *sécurité*—for safety.

We do not own a car. We walk where we need to go in the village. To go to Marseille we have the red bus which *le patron* calls his limousine. He waves to the driver and it stops for us. "Why own a car if we can command such a thing?" he says with a laugh. "With the bus I am Caesar!" Our home is a small flat. We rent, we do not own. Of all our acquaintances, only Mon. Papizan, the vendor of ice cream owns his flat.

Le patron does several exhibition dives every year. It is hard, but he likes the excitement, the applause. He is proud of the money he is able to raise this way to help the *incapacitateds*. He can tell you how many wheelchairs he has contributed. He keeps none of the contributions for himself.

Though he is not a priest his private discipline is very strict. There is the Yoga exercise he does for an hour every morning and the cold water he bathes in, but his discipline is more than that. He works constantly to keep his body and his mind strong. He is not one of the dissipated ones.

He follows the hard discipline because he once came too close to the edge. He almost lost control of himself. When I asked him what lies over the edge, he said, "Alcohol, drugs, violence, and the ruin of others which is worse than death." His faith and the discipline keep him safe from all that.

I was still a small puppy riding on his arm most of the time when it came the day of the dive. I did not know what was going on when he started up the tower.

I yelled that he should come down. I tried to follow him up. If you know about ladders you will understand why I could not do it. He went up and up. The sun was bright. The crowd was yelling encouragement and applauding, but as he got closer to the top the crowd quieted. Then it grew silent. I barked and howled with all my might. I jumped at the ladder. I knew something terrible was going to happen. I could smell the fear in the people. Their faces were twisted with it. Nobody spoke to me. They could not hear me.

Jean-Michel jumped.

He hit the water with his hands before him like an arrow. He was under for a long time. When he surfaced there were cheers.

The Officer of *Affaires Maritimes* was on duty in his boat. He pulled *le patron* out of the water. Jean-Michel waved. The cheering went on. They wrapped him in a white towel and carried him to the port.

He was OK, but I think the jumps have affected his hearing. I have more and more work to do now when the telephone rings or someone comes to the door. He has never mentioned it but I think his big jumps have deafened him.

Now when he dives he ties me to the ladder and raises his hand that I should remain still. I am almost calm when he ascends. Of course I bark to encourage him, to tell him that I am proud. I cannot help myself for that. He says he can hear the pride and encouragement in my voice. He says it helps his resolution to be strong in doing the one thing that scares him. He says he feels most alive in this fear.

It is strange, but I think he is addicted to his one fear. It has the power of a drug on him—like the fear of loss on the gambler. It is the ultimate stimulant. I worry that it will cause his end.

Le patron dives for occasions, for *fêtes* to aid the handicapped children. His dives into the Seine at

Paris are for occasions to raise money. He says that the river has a foul odor, but I think that is because it is fresh and he is used to salt.

He also swims in the cold water at Christmas to show people that it can be done. When he swims in the cold water I join him for the rescue. We are both hardened to it.

I have not mastered the high diving, but I will go off the lighthouse pier—a higher dive than any other dog on the port will attempt!

The schools send us our students. The children are 7 to 10 years old, boys and girls. When they first arrive they are silly. We have to be very strict with them. We are responsible. There are the dangers of being on the water, and there is only so much time—the 9 A.M. lesson must be complete by noon; the 2 P.M. lesson must end at 4:30. Any fooling around could lead to a delay or a capsize. It has happened. Then I really go to work!

They must learn the importance of the weather, so for one of the early lessons we march in a sharp line like sailors on parade to *Le Bureau des Affaires Maritimes* in the small stone building at the head of the port.

We introduce ourselves to the gruff M'sieur Pinet who was a *Notaire* once but now composes the weather map. He is a solid, square man with a square head and squared-off hair. He is only a little older than *le patron*. His features are cut sharp like an eagle's. He frightens the children when he shouts "*Entrez! Entrez!*" but he is not angry. He is one of the *incapacitateds*. He wears a boot on one leg to make it longer. He uses a brace to get about. He explains the winds, the clouds, what front is coming.

What do you eat? Do you eat fish? Cheese? Ham? I eat fish and cheese and ham. Eggs sometimes, the remains of the *cassoulet* on Sunday evening. And sausage. I have to eat strongly to keep my weight. Food is part of our national philosophy. Our most famous chief has declared, "Tell me what you eat and I will tell you what you are." The finest bellies on the port belong to our philosophers.

When he thinks of it, Alan brings me a treat of beef kidney in his back pack. As those packages leak and the scent is strong, the fragrance of beef kidney has worked into the brocade of his *sac*.

When he arrives I always give it a good sniff and nuzzle to see if he has remembered something for me.

Do you like coffee? Our French coffee is famous. It is better than our wine, which I do not care for. The best coffee is *la noisette*, a shot of espresso with steamed cream and a large lump of sugar. I empty *le patron*'s cup whenever I can.

Your Chairman is taken with the fragrance of our cigarettes. He follows behind a smoker seeking a strong whiff like I follow a ripe bitch. I think he has purchased a package of the *Gauloise*. Was he a smoker? Many who have sworn off smoking resume when they come into our sea air, taste this wine and catch the fragrance of our tobaccos. Those things go together.

In my next I will tell you about our *fête* of the Sacred Heart, which is coming up.

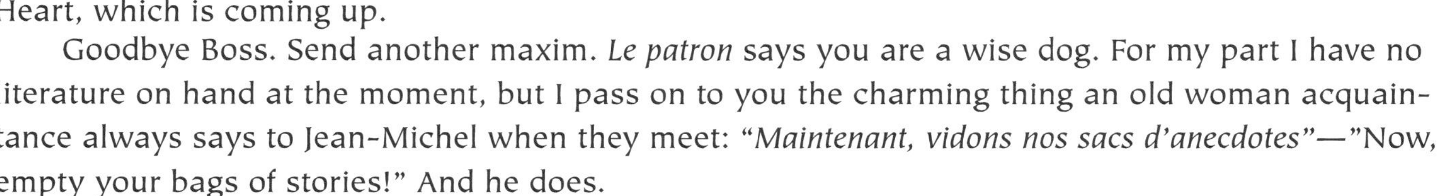

Goodbye Boss. Send another maxim. *Le patron* says you are a wise dog. For my part I have no literature on hand at the moment, but I pass on to you the charming thing an old woman acquaintance always says to Jean-Michel when they meet: "*Maintenant, vidons nos sacs d'anecdotes*"—"Now, empty your bags of stories!" And he does.

Regards,
Rodeo

PS—A poodle here has your mixed coloring and must be about your size. I pointed him out to Alan. He said your gait is different. This poodle is named Niger. Alan says that name would never go where you are because it sounds like what is a rude word with you showing great disrespect, and it is not P.C. What is P.C.?

June 10, Hatfield

Monsieur Rodeo—

Sweet days here. The potatoes blooming smell like lindens. I think about writing you and I look around with fresh eyes.

A dog joke for you: A Russian peasant in 1912, astonished by the telephone which he has just seen and heard for the first time, asks his educated friend Ivan how it works.

"The thing is simple," says Ivan. "Imagine a dog so large that it stretches from Moscow to Odessa. You step on the dog's tail in Moscow and it barks in Odessa. You see that much?"

The peasant squints as if to see. He nods a little.

"Good!" says Ivan. "Now remove the dog."

When Alan is here our daily work begins with a trip at 6 A.M. to the village for the *Times*. They won't do home delivery in our zip code, so we have to go off every morning to buy it at the Dairy Mart. I ride in the bicycle basket. For his last birthday Martha gave Alan the bicycle, a broad-tired one with black frame and chrome fenders, coaster brakes and no gears. It is cushy, heavy and slow—perfect for his age and this flat land.

His mounting and dismounting are not elegant. I clutch as the bicycle rocks and swerves, but once underway we throb along steadily like a pelican in flight. The chocolate Lab across the street who is kept in by an invisible electric fence pretends to rush us when we set out, but I bark and Alan rings the two-tone bell and she smiles and gives a friendly wag for a safe journey. This is her diversion.

Then Dan, the podgy corgi at #90 swings down all fluffed-up and noisy, so we call warnings and ring the bell and detour to the other side of the road. Not because we're afraid; Dan's eyesight is failing and we don't want to hit him.

Sandy at the Dairy Mart always saves a *Times* for us. She's a large, puffing woman who follows the crime stories. The closer the mayhem the happier she is. She longs for a stick up. She and Alan exchange how-are-yous and discuss crime and the weather. Then he stuffs the paper under his belt at the back. If the weather's nice we go on for an hour up the valley, seven miles to Whately and the bridge to Sunderland. There is a little mountain there called Sugarloaf, but it's not white, it's red and green. That's where we turn around. As we pedal along we greet the older ladies out taking their exercise together and the farmers surveying their fields. The ladies are always in a party, the men are always alone. If there's a tag sale we stop and check the books. When there's spinach or zucchini on the "honor system" tables by the road we pick up what we'd like for lunch. The air is sweet in the morning when we ride, fragrant with the smell of growing plants and earth. For our voyages we carry water, oranges, and a can of sardines. I love sardine oil.

Back home the first things we read are the obituaries—not for anyone we know but because that's the best-written part of the paper. Life stories are more interesting than anything. Curious that they always report what the deceased died of, even the old ones; it's not enough to say, "She died of old age." They have to give heart failure or cancer. Loneliness and heartache are never mentioned. The oldest ones are always the women. We have books of obituaries on the book van. And crime stories, murders and mysteries, but Alan doesn't read them. Tom says he has tastes to grow into.

In the late afternoon we bicycle again, this time to the town which is a bigger place than our village, to Starbucks for a coffee and then to the local shops and fleamarkets and to The Salvation Army store to look for books. I'm known to the girls at Starbucks and to all the booksellers. Many of them keep Milk Bones for me, and a dish of water in the summer. To preserve their figures the Starbucks girls give me the squares of butter that go with their scones. Butter is my favorite food in all the world. I like the salted best. In this I am like your opera singers!

On our way to town we pass a dog friend, a large black shepherd named Fremont. He looks fierce but he's a pussycat at heart. His hips are giving out. Alan is sympathetic. When we set out he tucks two Milk Bones in the band of his underwear, one for Fremont, one for me.

Fremont greets us with a smile and rushes for a stick, the longer and more unwieldy the better. Sticks and bicycles don't mix, so Alan stops, fishes out the Milk Bones, and we have a chat. Then Alan tosses the stick—only a little distance in deference to the condition of Fremont's hips—and we go on.

But one day Fremont wasn't there, so Alan never had a chance to stop and pass out the dog biscuits. After coffee and the bookstores we went to the "Y". Alan started to strip in front of his locker. Two men were talking together in front of the lockers opposite. They stopped when the Milk Bones fell out.

When he gets home I will encourage him to switch from Milk Bones to beef kidney!

What does it look like where you live? Where we live there are low furry mountains that are worn down and old and appear purple in this season. Along the river there are fields for tobacco, potatoes, and cucumbers. Along the roads where we ride the bicycle there are daisies and sweet rocket and wild iris, which have a strange scent and are called "bearded ladies," which is a pretty odd name. Right now the grass is in bloom and the scent is sweet, almost overwhelming when it rolls over you on a hot breeze.

There's a bar across the street from us, The Paddock Pizza. It is not like your cafés. Nobody sits outside. The idea of a bar here is that you hide inside. The only windows are little slits to reveal the blue and red neon beer signs which glow at a distance like Christmas lights. On Friday and Saturday nights a little of the dance music drifts over and that's nice, but when the boys who do not have dates go off they make their pickups roar. Sometimes they lose control and take out our mailbox. There are hot words then!

We have 2,000 Postal Patrons in our town. Not everybody gets mail every day, so our Postmistress can tell you if Ruth Brown got a letter. Why it is important if she did or didn't, I don't know, but yesterday when we were in the P.O. that was the talk. The Postmistress knows us, but she is formal in her work and doesn't chat because she's the boss. Fran and Dave who work with her always have a word for us about the weather and some bit of town gossip—the most interesting news. At Christmas we take them the grape jelly we make, bitter stuff to my taste but they pretend to be delighted because everybody likes to get a present, even something useless: it is a token of respect. Dogs understand this better than people.

Hatfield is mostly farms. The big property owners are the Polish farmers. At Easter they hang bright plastic eggs in their trees. The older men wear their hair cut to a grey burr. The farmer who owns the big place near us has a barrel belly and a small head. His guts jiggle when he walks. He's important at Town Meeting because, as Chaz the barber says, "The farmers own this town." Chaz has a lock on the farmers—he's cut their hair for fifty years and gotten all their gossip. He cuts Alan's hair and lets him know how the tobacco crop is doing. It takes about two minutes with the clippers and Alan comes out looking like a Polish farmer.

Only a few blacks live here, but in mid-May the crews arrive from Jamaica to plant and tend the tobacco. When they're around there are other bicyclers to wave at and we're all pretty cheerful on the road. Some of the black bicyclers play their radios loud as they go along. The local station plays polkas, so that's what we hear. At dusk you'll find a couple of those black men at the pay phone outside the Dairy Mart calling home to Jamaica.

You seemed to wonder in your last why we work so hard for our masters, why we even allow ourselves to be petted. It is because we were on earth before them. They are our children. We serve for joy, not out of necessity or gratitude. Gratitude is merely a sense of favors yet to come. The difference between humans and dogs is the thumb. With their thumb they make tools. From generation to generation they accumulate their tricks with tools, so they have automobiles, airplanes, bombs and computers. As their stock of tricks builds they forget their feelings for one another. It is for us to remind them of feeling.

As for Alan's interest in the War, someone on your coast saved a girl named Ellen. She was a protester in Germany, or someone in her family was, and she got in trouble for it. She had to escape. She ended up in Alan's family home in Maryland. Ben is going to ask Alan's Aunt Margie about this—she is the only old one left—but it will be difficult. Margie lives in another town, she does not hear well, and she doesn't like to talk about the War. Her favorite aunt was an opera singer in Vienna, and to keep singing she collaborated, or so the family says. It wasn't political with her, she just wanted to sing while she had a voice. Any mention of the War makes Margie touchy that somebody's going to get on the subject of her aunt, so Ben will have a hard time with her. War weaves into everything.

There are even traces of war here in Hatfield. War is part of life, but most dogs could go a lifetime without a fight. Four cannons from the Revolutionary War are aimed out towards the river from the front of the Library. The Library is cramped and poor, but those cannons are kept well painted. In the graveyard the Revolutionary War dead have markers with plastic flowers. Every Memorial Day they are remembered with fresh plastics, which reminds me of a description of a graveyard—"a garden in which the labels come up instead of the flowers."

The state history sign on our road reports that King Phillip's War was fought around here in the 1670s. He was an Indian, the sachem of his tribe. He lost, but as he went down he took out a lot of the village. Nothing from that time remains except the land—which is all that war was about anyway.

The bigger towns in New England have monuments with the names of boys who went south during the Civil War, and the places where they died. And every village, even the smallest, has its American Legion hall with old fieldpieces out front. One Legion Post near our place in Vermont has a tank. How they got it there I can't imagine.

But mostly the traces of war here are the people. The old men with their triumphs to tell, the ones from Vietnam who have nothing to say, the Poles who came here to escape war.

We had a boundary fight 300 years ago. The Governor tried to settle it with a letter to his opponent. "What does it all come to," he wrote at the end, "but greater and smaller dishes of porridge and 'Come, will you smoke it?'" (Meaning the peace pipe.) "If I perish, I perish. 'Tis but a bubble burst, a dream vanished. Eternity will pay for all."

That's about as far back as we go, not counting the dinosaurs. This land was a seabed once which is why our soil is so fine and silty. The sea was fresh water and dinosaurs came to its banks to drink. I've seen their footprints in stone. I am the length of a dinosaur foot.

A flap in the paper today: The American Kennel Club just published its *Complete Dog Book* with some ugly truths about daschunds, Dalmatians and Scottish terriers. Howls have gone up, lawsuits are threatened. "Not good for children" is the comment on small poodles, which sounds right to me, but the entries on Doberman pinschers and bull terriers offended, and the clubs of Maltese terriers, borzois, Chihuahuas and whippets have raised such a ruckus that the "Canine Bible" has been withdrawn at a cost of $800,000 to the A.K.C. The howler in all this is that most family dogs don't fall under any of the classifications anyway since they're mixed breeds. By the way, are you pedigreed? You haven't said.

You asked what a Foundation is. They are usually set up in the ruins of a great estate by a rich person who pays for everything so he can ride his hobby horse and amuse his friends and flatterers while absorbing their gossip and their reputations. The food is good, the wine excellent, and the provider of all avoids his income tax. Few of the guests do serious work since they must prepare all day to glitter in the evening and secure their next invitation.

You wanted another maxim. Here's one of Poor Richard's: "The best service to God is kindness to one's fellow men, but prayer is easier and therefore preferred."

Here comes Ben!

Compliments to *le patron* and a lick for Alan.

Jefe

June 20, Cassis

Dear Ben—

Looming out of the mist this morning, an American battleship and a French minesweeper here to help us celebrate the *fête de la mer* this weekend. Last night the late bus from Marseille brought the girls marching in to do their part. The fishing boats are gay and gaudy with swooping lines; the warships are gray and awkward.

I went down for my newspaper about eleven. Two sailors were filming each other—sound video—talking about the heat, the girls on the beach, the girls on the port.

"What's the name of your ship?" I asked the black sailor.

"*The Mitcher*."

"Armed?"

"You bet! Tomahawk missiles, 5" guns, enough stuff to take out a small country."

The *petits marins* were out. Suddenly Rodeo was in full voice and the kids were singing their school song. The dozen tiny sailboats had circled *The Mitcher*. She was their prisoner, Tomahawks and all. As Jean-Michel shouted his heathenish "*Ongawas*!" in the almost-no breeze, a tiny band of whitish lace with pink dots circled the gray lady's thigh.

We went out to Presqu'île yesterday. A few minutes after Martha got set up an old-style Harley came rumbling down the gravel track. First I noticed the driver's fine tanned legs, then the lizard boots and the frilly white ballerina's skirt, then the little dog. The black leather vest revealed a woman for sure as she wore nothing under it. The Harley had flames on its fenders.

As soon as she dismounted a few yards down, the Chihuahua took off on affairs of his own. I yelled for a photograph but maybe she didn't hear me.

My next visitor walked up wheeling his delicate blue racing bicycle. This road is too rough for it. He was a slim, dark gold boy, not tall, with thickly curled black hair. He wore a freshly pressed white T-shirt and curiously striped short pants with a flowered ribbon around the cuffs. He smiled a big smile and gestured to explain why he was not riding. He had fine white teeth.

I said a few words and he stopped for a visit. He was in no hurry. He was on his way to his boat. He lives on his boat in the *calanque*, but he can't go out sailing, his boat is too old, too decrepit, so he's rebuilding her. He knows Jean-Michel; Jean-Michel is his good friend who just got him a bargain set of used sails. The boy supports himself working for the Association that cleans the beaches with garbage bags and heavy gloves. He's been to Canada, traveled down the west coast from Vancouver to Guatemala. We switched to English. His English is fine.

At his neck he wears a tight black leather choker with three ambers bound in woven silver wire. He collects amber, studies and trades in it in a small way. "It was the first jewel," he explained,"the first thing the ancients wore." He wears it because it is warm. It protects him, he says. Whenever he's been down or broke he's been able to barter a piece of amber for what he needs. He'll show me some the next time we meet.

His name is Erez. He spelled it out for me—"Cedar in Hebrew," he said. He's Israeli, "but my grandmother was from Sicily, which is why I am a little bit black." He's twenty-eight, on his own since he was sixteen. He looks sixteen. "I am very light in my living. I have myself, my boat and my bicycle," he laughed. "I am a wanderer." And he was gone.

Later we walked out to the *calanque* where he ports his boat. We found his bicycle but no sign of a ramshackle sailboat. There was a dinghy at one mooring. Perhaps he managed a sail after all. Hope we run into him again. I'd like to see his boat and how he lives. He's original.

I got a haircut. It took three women two hours and $40 to do it. Do you remember the child's story about Dandelion the lion who had his hair cut before the party and came out looking so strange, so fluffed-up and rare that nobody at the party recognized him, so they wouldn't let him in? It was like that. I bought a palm-weave hat with a black band to make up for certain shortcomings.

Yesterday to the public laundry with shopping bags leaking our month's worth of dirty clothes. To parade along the port with that cargo is humbling. The casino dudes stare with disdain, their babes with pity. How they do their laundry I don't know, but then they don't wear much beyond gold chain and tan.

People walking by the Laverie Wash Matiq always look in to see who's there, what stuff is displayed. People go by the grocery and the clothing shop without a glance, but the laundry gets a long peer. It is a little embarrassing to be seen in there by anyone you know, like being seen going over the help-wanted ads. We investigate each other in the laundry, curious to see the underwear, the shirts, the sheets, their quality and state of repair. French underwear is the best, the most expressive, the most hopeful.

People in the laundry follow a code. You start your wash and then go shopping or read by the fountain, secure that no one will take your carrying bag or pinch your soap. If the dryer finishes before you return and someone is waiting, that person will fold your things.

While our stuff was gurgling and banging away, I went to Marie Laurant's to buy our fish. Marie was sitting outside the shop on her bench in the sun, her back against the cool side wall. She's tanned and whiskery. Her smile warms the heart.

This time she didn't get up. She called inside to the fisherman who was helping her out. "The heat," she explained, laughing as she talked. "It makes me tired!" She stretched out her legs in the warm. She wears old boots. Her legs are dark and lumpy, bruised-looking. The *pêcheur* with the dead stump cigar in his mouth found the right sole and skinned it. No knife, he just peeled it like opening a mango and gutted it with a quick finger. Marie heaved up to manage the money.

"I'm retiring," she said.

"Where?"

"Here. Right here. I'm retiring here."

Of course. How could she leave her bench, her friends that pass by with news, the *pêcheurs* she's known all her life? Her husband was a *pêcheur* until he started this shop. Inside there's a photograph of him with their daughter as a little girl, the two of them holding up a big fish. How could she leave the baker she goes to twice a day for gossip and her *baguette*?

How could she leave her mad sister-in-law Lucienne—the one they call *la fadade,* the mad one—the hunched-over hawk lady who sings for tips at the café tables and wanders around the port at night accosting strangers for money to buy a crust? She is said to own properties but we give her money. She looks desperate. When we hand her a coin she smiles and offers a song. She doesn't want to beg, she wants to earn. She has a sweet voice, clear like a girl's. She sings in the choir. But do not attempt a photograph. I did. She got furious.

She has a habit of scarfing bread from the baskets on the café tables. She's very quick but it startles the diners, so the waiters shoo her away. She snarls then, draws up close and yells into the man's face, "Would you treat your grandmother so?" The waiters shrug and turn away. To be rude to her would be to risk your eyes.

Anyway, Marie Laurant has the right idea. Stop in

your tracks when you're tired but stick around. Don't go away and leave what you've known, your friends, your ways, your place. Pass on the day-to-day work but stay put. Like Frances Steloff at the Gotham Book Mart. She sold the shop one day and showed up the next for work, went right back into her purple room at the rear with the mystics and her white cats. She died there. That's a perfect retirement. I want to settle in some Eden, build up my bookshop and sit out front in the sun until there's nothing left.

When it's cool Marie bellies up to the cutting table, wipes her hands on her dress and cuts and guts cheerfully. She's fast with squids, a potter with her clay. Her daughter helps out sometimes in jodhpurs and silk, but you can tell she's trying to keep the fish at a distance. She reads the fashion magazines out front while she smokes. She'll peel your fish but her heart isn't in it. Marie cleans fish the way Martha paints, uninhibited, full-bodied, the dancer in her dance.

The other morning Martha went down to the port. A boat was just in with flapping, gasping fish for sale. She bought two mottled reds with big eyes and savage mouths. The fisherman warned her about the spines. She told him she'd be OK, she'd bought them to paint. He looked dismayed and took something off the price. We now have two *roches* on canvas and two gaudies in the refrigerator. They're begining to taint the coffee. The spines carry poison.

The fish aren't the only thing tainting the coffee. Your mother is running short of turps. She's discovered that it settles out quickly in the *frigo*. You can imagine the rest. Our eggs and cheese range in flavor from pine to *poisson*.

Apéritifs at the Foundation a few nights ago where we met a native named Henri who speaks English, a lean, sharp-nosed man smartly turned-out and pretty macho—rides a motorcycle and talks a lot about France needing "a strong man" to run the government. He's 81, taut and straight-standing, but his mouth is going soft like an old woman's. He must look like his mother did when she was old.

He told us that the Germans scuttled a large ship in the harbor here to prevent an invasion.

They set up shore guns and machinegun nests along the shore. He explained that the little stone huts we see along the coast were part of their defenses. "We couldn't move!"

He was an engineer in the French merchant fleet. When the Germans commandeered it he quit. He was broke. He lived with his mother in Cassis. They had no food. He had no papers. He refused to register because many young men his age were sent to work in the forced labor camps in Germany. Others had to patrol sections of the railway at night. If a section was blown up its guard was shot.

He needed money. The French Navy office in Marseille put out a call for crews to move up to Marseille some French vessels that had been surrendered at Genoa and were blocking that port. The pay was good with no questions asked. A plus for him was that his German was good. The chief checked Henri's Navy record and he was signed up. His papers now were temporary ones of the *Kreigsmarin*—the German Navy. He was made Chief Engineer to return to service a large passenger boat.

He recruited a dozen ragtag merchant marine men on the lam like himself—"the scum, they were"—and took his crew by train to Genoa. They met their Captain and surveyed the vessel, a packet from the Marseille-IndoChina run. She'd lain idle for two years. Her pumps had seized, some parts had been cannibalized. When the Captain heard that it would take at least two months to put her back in service he took off to the country. He said they should call him when she had steam.

"Genoa was a dream then," Henri mused. "There was food, you could buy things. Here in the south of France there was nothing, the Germans kept it stripped for the homeland.

"One day in the street in Genoa I ran into a popular Italian movie actress. My aunt was famous in films in France before the War. This woman had visited her for French lessons. My aunt was very busy at the time of the visit so she had asked me to give the lessons and, by the way, to show this beautiful Italian actress a good time. I'd done my best, and there she was, calling to me from across the street! I tell you, for three months it was *la dolce vita*!

"But the ship parts—where was I to get the parts I needed to repair the packet? I could not send to Marseille, there was nothing there.

"I called on the commander of the largest German ship in the port. I explained my problem—and his: 'If you want the port cleared of this thing, you must give me what I need to put her under steam.' He asked for a list of my requisitions. I had it in my pocket. He signed it, then took me to dinner in the officers' mess. We had wine, cognac and cigars. These men were educated, civilized. They were not Nazis. The German Navy was not Nazi.

"We had almost restored the vessel when I heard rumors that some of the other vessels that had been restored and gone off for Marseille—all much smaller than my packet—had been sunk on the way. Who sank them? Who could say. . .

"I decided to take the train back to Marseille to investigate. Also, we had not been paid and our Captain was not to be found. It fell to me to see to the affairs of my crew. I got to Marseille and scoured the harbor. I knew the names of the eight ships that had departed Genoa. Only three were in the harbor. I called on the officer who had given me my commission. I explained that the vessel was almost restored to service but we needed our pay, and what were we to do with her? We had no Captain, and she was so large a vessel, she would be a sitting duck for whomever was potshotting at ships progressing along the coast.

"He said, 'The Germans want her out of the port. She is ready to depart. We have done our part. Let them furnish the crew for her sailing to Marseille.' He gave me my pay and the money for my companions, and I returned to Genoa.

"We finished our work and fired the boilers. In two days we had steam and had tested the turbines. All was in readiness. We went shopping. We bought soap, oil and tinned food for home, and some delicate items of clothing for our special friends. But of course we would never be allowed to pass Customs with those goods. So we made up several large bundles and tagged each with the name of a *Kreigsmarin* officer.

"Then I called again on the German commander. I explained that all was in readiness, but we needed a crew. We had no crew. This surprised him very much. I told him that our Captain was not to be found. 'Ah,' he said. He understood that without a Captain we could do nothing, for that is the German way—but of course, had we wanted to, we twelve could have taken that packet anywhere. But, as it was, we had another excellent dinner together, he tucked two more cigars in my pocket for the journey, and the next morning my *copains* and I boarded the train for Marseille with our carefully tagged bundles of booty.

"At Customs there was no difficulty. A French customs man to question the property of a *Kreigsmarin*?" —Henri made the little spitting noise that is Provençal for contempt—"So my mother and I lived comfortably for a few months on those provisions, and I was popular with certain friends."

As he told all this Henri laughed and laughed. "The War, it was the best time of my life. We were young, we had friends, there was always wine and excitement. We lived at the edge. You do not need sleep when you live at the edge. "

"What was the edge?" I asked.

"The risk of death was close. We were never bored."

"You were in the *Resistance*?"

He looked up sharply, his clear blue eyes suddenly young and full of surprise, then anger. For an instant I could see the boy he had been.

He again made the Provençal *pfft* of dismissal and gestured as if he were tossing aside an annoyance.

"The *Résistants* were Communists. I was not Communist. I was not among the *maquis*, but some of them I knew. It was a long time ago. They are all dead."

This could be Ellen's place. Submarines slipped into the *calanques* on dark nights to supply the *maquis* and take people off. That much is local lore, but who the refugees were, and where they came from? I haven't found anyone who remembers or wants to. Henri's the closest I've come to someone who knows what went on, but he'll be a tough clam to open. He will not be pried.

It is now 4:30, the afternoon class is coming in, I hear Rodeo yelling instructions. I wish he'd bark the battleships off. I'm off to the port. I'm going to talk with Jean-Michel about going out with a class. Did you know I was a Sea Scout once? That was on the Potomac River. I was fifteen. No waves. Not much wind either.

A wag to the dog and an embrace for you.

Love, Dad

July 1, Hatfield

Dad—

I went to see Margie. She bucked and muttered that all this stuff should be dead and buried like the people who lived it, but I was able to piece together this much.

Ellen was picked up on the coast near Marseille in November '43. Who brought her down from Germany, Margie says she never heard, but the trip took months. They went in relays down the rivers, sometimes walking, sometimes in small boats. From Lyon south they always traveled by boat, a different one every night.

When they got to Marseille they hid her there for a month or six weeks, then hiked three nights to the pickup point. The hike was hard, mountains and no food. Ellen fell and broke her big toe. The pickup was by submarine, but English, American or Free French? Margie doesn't remember.

There were three in the group that escaped—Ellen, her brother, and another prisoner who led them south. Her brother died in the escape. Only Ellen made it to Gibraltar.

That's all Margie could remember.

Sandy at the Dairy Mart is in heaven. There was a stick up. She was in the papers. Kid up the street did it. They caught him in about half an hour. Toy gun.

Your dog is well and sends greetings. Did I tell you he has a love interest? Guinness, the ginger Lab down the street. Jefe will go that far and no further. He stands outside her screen door and barks. She barks from the other side. Tristan and Iseult. I've got four chapters done.

Ben

July 1, Cassis

Jefe my gallant—

A rude dog joke for you: What is the difference between a male dachshund and a street vendor? The street vendor bawls out his wares along the pavement, while the dachshund...

OK. Sorry! I must immediately tell you our large news here. We had a crisis at sea today. Jean-Michel says a casualty might have occurred but for my heroism.

It has been cloudy and rainy, odd weather for this season. The sea has been running very large swells. For two days we did not go out. The students practiced knots, cleaned the equipment lockers, checked the sails for tears—all that sort of make-work. They grew impatient. So did Jean-Michel.

Today the weather was no better, but Jean-Michel decided it would be OK to tow the boats to a sheltered cove off the Lombard and try a sail there. So the boats went out on a long line towed by *Zodiac*. The sailors were all instructed to keep low and hold on. The risk was the swinging boom. The boats pitched in the swells, but the swells came regularly and the children could see them coming.

We made it to the cove. The weather continued squally. When the boats were released the students were instructed to paddle in a large circle and allow *les cornes* to swing free so the sails would luff and not hold the wind.

We should never have allowed our little marines to step their masts, but *le patron* misjudged the weather. He knew it was going to be rough; he wanted the students to experience a sail in rough weather. That is when he likes to hold the races. But the weather soured, it worked up to *un orage*. The sky grew dark. *Le patron* ordered that we turn back. The children were scared and very serious. We were lucky with the painters, everything held, we started back to the port.

As we rounded the lighthouse jetty where the big rocks are—the breakwater—a luxury boat passed us coming in. In his fear of the storm—*le tonnerre* was sounding—the skipper had maintained more speed than is permitted there. He cast up a terrific wake.

In the confusion of the swells, the wake and the free-swinging *cornes*, one of our sailors rose up a little to be sick over the side. He was knocked overboard. Perhaps it was the pitch of the wake, perhaps he was struck by the boom.

I saw it all. I was in the water before the first yell went up.

Le patron could not maneuver immediately to collect the child because he had all the sailboats in tow and they were close to the rocks.

The child was afloat—the orange life vest saw to that—but he was gagging and choking on his sick. In his plunge I think he swallowed a lot of seawater.

I could see that the swells, the wake and the wind were driving the boy toward the rocks. I had to keep him out in the channel.

By now *le patron* was sounding an alarm on the air horn he carries—a warning that there is a serious accident at sea and all the boats in the area should be on alert to help with the rescue.

I got a good clamp on the back of the life vest, made sure the child's head stayed above water, and paddled with all my might into the main channel. I tell you, I have never swum so hard in my life—and with my neck twisted to tug! All the while the child flailed at me with his arms, gagging and being sick.

"To the shore! To the shore!" he would yell when he caught breath enough—little realizing that if we'd drawn close to the shore at that spot the swells and wake would have dashed us against the breakwater.

Because of *le patron*'s air-horn warnings no boats

cruised in the channel. He had pulled over to one of the boats docking in the port and handed the skipper the painter to the string of sailboats.

Then he zoomed to us in *Zodiac*, dragged the child out of the water and held him upside down to drain him like you would empty a pail of fish guts. After that he pumped him roughly in the bottom of the boat and stuck his fingers down the child's throat to make him vomit. Only when he was sure the boy was breathing properly did he reach over for me.

"Rodeo!" he said. "You are a hero today."

The whole affair did not last ten minutes but it seemed like hours.

Later we walked to M'sieur Prévot's *boucherie* where a large beef kidney was selected. In its white suet case it was the size of a soccer ball. M'sieur Prévot sliced it open with a pleasing sound like a zipper opening, and there lay the kidney, red as rubies and jiggling in the light. It was all mine.

Le patron reported the skipper of the speeding luxury boat to the Officer of *Affaires Maritimes*. That skipper will suffer a large fine. *Le patron* says perhaps his privilege of mooring at Cassis will be suspended.

Now I am lying on our porch. I can see the nightly party boat to Corsica on its way out from Marseille. It looks like one of your skyscrapers lying on its side, it has so many lights. It is all *de luxe*— the music and dancing, the tinkle of glasses as in one of our best restaurants here, the women in their fragrances, the gambling. I can't see or hear those things, but I can picture them.

I am very tired or I would tell you about our *fête de la mer*. Another letter. *A bientôt* Jefe

Regards,
Rodeo

July 4, Hatfield

Mariner the Hero!

Hurrah for your quick work at sea! That boy will remember you with many toasts when he tells his story. I've told your American Gang here all about it. Max and Guiness barked with pride for you! Of course, there may come a time when the man who tells it recalls that he saved you. That is the way they remember.

By comparison to yours my life seems dull and ordinary. Your fine letters flatten me—they are so rich in events, rarities, affairs of the world. How can I respond? With A&M gone there've been no outings for painting, and the book van sits rusting. Tom quotes Robert Burton's truth, "For Peregrination charmes our senses with such unspeakable and sweet variety, that some count him unhappy that never travelled, a kinde of prisoner, and pitty his case that from his cradle to his old age beholds the same still; still, still the same, the same."

This is our Independence Day. Our American Legion Post is hung with bunting, rosettes and colored lights like a store at Christmas. At town expense we have new flags around Hatfield Center, and for a week the booms have been building up. Only a few at first so you think it's a thunderstorm coming, but it's just the boys testing their cherry bombs. On the 4th old soldiers fire off their 45s, but not the Vietnam vets. They don't celebrate.

Ben tells me there is a love of France in France, that your patriotism is not political. Ours is the property of the right, a political stance. There's no strong, warm "love of country" feeling here right now. Our patriots are all against something.

Anyway, the explosions hurt my ears. They're like thunder, the thing I'm most afraid of, I don't know why. I hear it and all my strength goes out in a rush. I can barely crawl to shelter.

We've had flyovers by the National Guard boys in their gleaming F-16s making a display for the folks at home, and a slow parade of the truly huge black cargo planes based at Westover—the C5As which can deliver a load of tanks and trucks anywhere in the world on command. The screaming of their engines on a low pass is worse than sirens. Every time there's a troop buildup somewhere we know it before the newspapers report it. We can't tell you where, but we know it's happening. They are sinister, those monsters.

The corn fields are dark green and knee-high, the tobacco is flourishing. The big money and the

big risk are in tobacco. They plant it in stages, seedling by seedling, so if a heavy thunderstorm or hail knocks down one crop they'll have another. Hail is the greatest peril. It doesn't bother the corn so much, but if a tobacco plant gets battered it dies. And blue mold. Overnight, blue mold can take out a whole field.

I chew grass sometimes but not tobacco. I tried it once. My heart raced, my ears buzzed, I thought I'd fly off the earth. Why chewing it doesn't kill them I don't know, but it sure makes for good ballplayers. The crews that work it are mostly black because green tobacco gives the whites a rash.

The moment the plants stop growing and start to flower they're cut and hung upside down to dry in long barns with many tall doors on the sides to aid the drying. Last year there was no hail and only a little blue mold, the crop fetched $9 a pound and there were new Fords at Christmas and trips to Florida.

On the bench outside Chaz's Barber Shop now the tobacco farmers talk about the crop. The largest farmer—our Big Cheese of tobacco whose belly does a little dance when he walks—holds a cigar wrapped in a leaf he grew, but as it cost him $10 he just holds it, he doesn't smoke it. It's the same one he waved around last year. For all his Polish name, he's Yankee to the core and thrift is his religion. His maxim is "Use it up, wear it out, make it do, do without." There's no play in the Big Cheese.

The other main maxim here is "Waste not, want not," so nobody throws anything out. Worn clothes recycle from yard sale to yard sale, and old machinery rusts where it died. Bicycling around, you can follow the history of trucks and tractors back eighty years.

Cukes are ripe. Night and day the cucumber-picker's going. Labor's tight even with the migrants, and wages are high, so Martha's niece works on it. She goes to college off and on. She's smart and chunky, careless about how she looks or what she says. She's a geek to the college boys around, but the lonely Jamaicans she works with love her.

The machine they ride is a ramshackle wing that spans ten rows. The pickers—six or eight of them—lie on their bellies snatching up ripe cukes as the rig chugs along. At break time Cybele sketches her friends, at night they dance before tumbling like puppies together into a heap of tired. Mountains of cucumbers come off our fields.

It's a custom here that the young men declare their intentions by drawing a large heart and writing their initials and those of their beloveds in white paint on the side of a barn. This can be seen from the road. You can follow a fellow through three or four affairs this way if you travel around on the bicycle as we do. Of course no Lothario ever uses the same barn twice, and the whitewash doesn't last long, so there are no embarrassing reminders. Sometimes they're moved to poetry. "Should the sun refuse to shine/ Ruth you'd still be mine" is the latest.

Boys and men do most of our wall writing, but one jilted girl got mad enough to leave a note. Under what must have been her defaulted Galahad's declaration she wrote, "Sam is sludge."

Rodeo, in one of your letters you mentioned my grandchildren. I have no grandchildren. When I was about six months old they performed the operation on me. I'm a gelding. The idea was that I would be more content this way. I'm not. In my mind when I catch the scent of a bitch in heat I'm as concupiscent as a bull terrier. The frustration has affected my temper.

The fact of my condition is obvious enough, but you're the only one I've ever mentioned it to. I wouldn't mention it at all if we lived face to face, but distance has the effect of a strong drink on inhibitions. And, as you say, everything is permitted in a correspondence.

We have an eccentric in Hatfield. He's known for his hat. He just passed on the sidewalk in his orange stocking cap and black leather jacket—the same rig he wore in January when it was -17F. Today it's 90. He's thin, hunched over, not tall, 30-something. Our Ichabod or Uriah—he must have a name like that—won't speak or engage eyes. Sometimes when we're out on the bicycle we see him hoeing the tobacco plants in his plot. Or we think it's his plot. It's behind the old house that's going to ruin that we see him coming out of. Does he live alone? Is he with his parents?

Once I saw him pull off his cap and toss his fine long hair as if he were drying it. It was beautiful hair, auburn colored, which is rare with us, long and silky like a girl's. Then he gathered it up and stuffed it back under his orange camouflage. Maybe he sings in a rock band.

He always returns from his daily walk with a small bag. Its outline suggests a quart of milk and a few other things. His pace is always the same, an odd balls-of-the-feet rocking-along gait. Max says he walks like he's got an egg up his ass. We all bark but it doesn't do any good.

But for the quarantine I would have come along to France to help Martha at her work. Usually when she goes out I go along to guard. She watches the landscape so intently, she doesn't notice things. She's like the cat you can creep up on as it waits for its prey. I lie close by and growl if anyone approaches.

The problem ones are the men who presume to advise. The more she ignores them the louder they bellow their wisdoms. Parties of older women out walking are difficult too. They'll crowd around and ask questions. She pretends not to hear, but once or twice as if in alarm she's turned on them swiftly with a dripping brush. *Then* they scurry!

Sometimes Alan poses. This is hard work because once Martha starts painting he can't move or she'll lose the motif and have to start over. She scolds if he shifts in his chair. I've never been asked to sit. Bonnard painted his dachshund in a picture with a woman drinking coffee and called the painting "Coffee." Do you think that was the dog's name?

I like the smells of painting, the turps and oils. Any time I catch a whiff I'm back home like Proust with his biscuit. New paintings leak a fragrance that's reminiscent of being in a pine wood on a hot afternoon. It's strongest in the studio. One snort in there ruins your nose for hours.

I go as guard dog when she takes her paintings to New York. She shows in a gallery in SOHO, which is the district of painters. The people there keep dogs, many of them rare, but they're so busy with their painting and their work on the telephones that five or six dogs must be taken out together by a person who's hired to walk them. I like the company of other dogs but I wouldn't like sharing a leash.

What's most peculiar about this arrangement is that the man who minds their leash must collect their duties in a plastic bag— which I would find embarrassing. The life of the New York dog is very different from mine in the country and yours by the sea.

When Martha is visiting the galleries and museums with her work, Alan and I walk the streets of SOHO and visit the bookshops. Stolen books are sold cheap off tables on the street, so we stop at those tables. And there are the out-of-prints in the shops. Alan likes to sell all kinds of books, but especially books of natural history. They're not popular with the New York readers, so we can always find things for Zora.

Our prize last trip was a 1931 *Outline of Natural History* for a dollar. It has a chapter on "Instinct and Intelligence Among Mammals" which gives an account of Lord Avebury's dog who could read cards marked "Out" and "Tea." Why they find this remarkable I don't know, but get this: "We must not be too generous in thinking over this kind of behaviour; the dog had simply learned to link together in its mind certain black marks and certain desirable things, such as a walk or a meal."

I asked Alan, "So how did *you* learn to read?"

At dusk in SOHO in the bars and bistros it is the women you see talking slow and long together, not the men. The men belt back their drinks and move on. They always have more work to do with pieces of paper, calls to make on their pocket telephones. Then we pass the bars where the gay men sit. They have time to talk. They have time for pleasure and art. Without them who would do the painting and music and writing and run the galleries?

I love Hatfield but I come to life in New York. It works on me like coffee. Your town, being much larger than my village, must have the same effect on you. Your letters glitter with things going on. In Hatfield we have only the quiet rhythms of the farms. Sometimes it's so quiet a cricket can startle you.

Do you know your parents? I know the names of mine because I am pedigreed: I am the son of Black Dancer out of Chocolate Momma, but I never knew them. I was born in North Dakota, which is in Red Indian country. At a fragile age I was shipped east to a kennel in New Jersey that specializes in poodles. That's where the family found me.

At that moment they were desperate for a puppy. They'd had a poodle named Killer. He was a nervous dog, hard to control. One day on a morning walk for his duties something startled him, he slipped his leash and got hit by a car. Alan rushed to pick him up. The driver stopped. They were both shocked. There was no blood, but the dog was limp. The blow had snapped his spine. He couldn't breathe. He died in Alan's arms. At the moment of death his breath came out in a long howl.

That evening they came to my kennel. I'd only been there a few days. The family loved me from the start, but before I could go home with them I had to have a bath and a poodle clip. The lady dried me with a hair dryer, which was very unpleasant, then she tied a blue ribbon on my head. I looked ridiculous, "A black balloon with a blue string," Ben laughed. I haven't had a poodle cut since. I'm cut to look like a rat terrier.

Last week we drove up to Vermont, about an hour north, to say hello to Tom and put in at the cabin for a couple of days. Tom's been doing poorly, so Mary is loading him up with zinc and wheat juice to revive his zip. Maybe what she feeds him is causing the problem. He was reading *The Merchant of Venice* when we arrived and right off gave us this from memory:

The world is still deceiv'd with ornament.
In law, what plea so tainted and corrupt
But, being season'd with a gracious voice,
Obscures the show of evil? In religion,
What damned error but some sober brow
Will bless it, and approve it with a text,
Hiding the grossness with fair ornament?
There is no vice so simple but assumes
Some mark of virtue on his outward parts.

Tom sent us off with a copy of the play. It's always like that with him—he presses his enthusiasms on you but he never seems to run out. His shelves get fuller and fuller. Imagine if he were a banker.

Then we drove up the long hill to the cabin where the mice have been making free and Cimba, the razorback across the road, has marked my territory. I quickly took care of Cimba. As for the mice, they've been eating the soap of Marseille and making nests in the sweaters. The nests would be OK if they didn't shred the sweaters as they settle in. One good Irish wool now has a ragged hole. Ben decided we had to chuck it, so the lady mouse and her babies and their fancy duvet were carefully laid in a carton and put in the woodshed. She has a family of five, each about the size of my toe, pink and hairless. I sniffed them carefully. They smelled sweet. They were warm and blind.

Already the mice are laying in hoards of seeds, neat little piles sorted by size and color. Those were among the shirts and underwear, but they caused no trouble so we didn't touch them.

For excitement we had a bear. Ben was reading on the deck; I was dozing. I caught a strange scent like rancid fat, then I saw him. He was not a big one as bears go, perhaps twice your size. Our smell gave him no concern. Only when I barked a good strong "Shoo!" did he begin to gallop, front feet between rear. He looked like a bouncing black ball then. He had long yellow claws. Ben was surprised. He hadn't seen a bear here before. The bear was black and shiny.

The people here used to eat them. English merchants would import young bears and fatten them with dumplings and sugar before serving them up like lambs. When they shoot a bear here now they don't eat it, they save the fat for a tonic against baldness. Baldness is a big problem with the men here, but not the women. Do Frenchmen go bald? Why are the women spared? Have you ever run into a bald dog?

While we were in Vermont, the wind came up and stirred the pines so they sounded like water. I imagined that I was there on the Mediterranean with you toasting on the port after a vigorous class with many races and cheers and your barking the *Allez*! and the *Giddyup Ongawa*! I've been practicing a four-beat bark myself—very distinctive. My voice is singular enough in tone, but developing a special vocabulary for warnings and encouragements seems a pretty good idea, and "Ongawa!" sure surprises my friends.

At sunset when the deer came by for the tender grass shoots they like so much I gave them the "*Allez*!" They were startled, but they didn't stir. They know me.

From the telephone calls he's been making—and he is not one to make telephone calls—I gather Ben has a serious lady interest. Plans are being made. This will come as a surprise to Martha and Alan. They'll be pleased. They worry that he's a loner, "the cat that walks alone," his grandmother calls him. It's time, he's 30. That's about the limit for being able to make a life with someone; much more time on your own and it can only be your life and her life like two roads running parallel with crossovers now and then. Anyway, all I know is that she has two cats, Geronimo and Jones, both capons and large as meatloafs. I have no interest in meeting them.

I have a riddle for you, pal:

Four stiff-standers
Four dilly-danders
Two lookers, two crookers
And a wig-wag.

What is it?

And a dog joke:

Man goes with mutt to a Talent Agent.
Man: "I got a talking dog here."
Agent: "Yeah yeah. We get one a week."
"No, really, this dog can talk."
He turns to his dog: "What's sandpaper feel like?"
"Rough!"
Agent groans and waves at the door.
Man: "What's on top of a house?"
"Roof!"
Agent, rising from desk with a heavy object, "Out!"
Man, running, "Greatest baseball player in all time?"
"Ruth!"
Object is thrown.
Dog to injured man in elevator: "DiMaggio?"
A while back you asked what is "P.C." I asked Ben. He says it is like a first cereal for babies, a

thing that comes out in the same state that it went in: a work of art that does not interest, excite, arouse, amuse, irritate or interest anyone. Most artwork paid for by grants, endowments and Foundations is P.C.

He told me "Jack and the Beanstalk" in P.C.: no giant, no big stalk, and Jack and the old lady who helped him steal go to jail.

My maxim for today is, "Change is the remedy for the ills of life."

My best to you and G & O—

Jefe

July 15, Cassis

My Friend Jefe, Sachem of Hatfield—

Glad for yours of Independence Day. Yesterday we celebrated the start of our Revolution with the same explosions and parades. The mayors all worked themselves up to a fine frenzy for their patriotic speeches. The port was hung with little plastic *tricolores* that snap and rattle in the wind. The communists celebrate one France, the socialists another, the *Front National* celebrate a country without Jews or Arabs. Our patriotism is not much different than yours. We blackfeet lie low on Bastille Day.

A bit of excitement here. It is the hot, dry season and there are often fires up in the forests.

Today the cutter of the Office of Affaires Maritimes raced out into the *Baie* to alert all the craft there to clear the area, the fire fighting planes were coming in for water. Jean-Michel led our fleet to the Lombard, where the water is shallow and protected.

About twenty minutes later, with a huge roar, two orange and black square-bellied prop jets lowered over the water as if they were going to land. Engines screaming, they skimmed the surface like dragonflies sucking huge mouthfuls of water into their holds. Then they nosed up suddenly with full bellies, their mouths leaking as the holds closed, to go dump the water on the fires.

I have only heard of this before.

The children waved and shouted at the brave pilots. Jean-Michel led them in shouting, waving his fists with the "*Giddyup! Ongawa!*" Today all of our sailors will become Forest Service pilots.

As with your July 4 addresses of the F-16s, we got the Mirage jets paying a courtesy to the town on their return to their base at Salon. They came in low over the *Baie* yesterday and dipped their wings. The noise was tremendous but the people at the cafés raised their glasses and cheered. Of course the people in the cafés along the port clutch their dogs when they hear the Mirages coming. Even so, a terrified Yorkie wound up in the harbor.

I am used to it, but the roar makes me lie down even in the bilge water. I had to lie down today when the Forest Service planes came over. The noise makes me helpless. I lose my strength. This sounds like what you experienced with the July 4 explosions.

Le patron says that our Mirage flyovers are not just for public entertainment, they carry a message for the Algerians here who might have sympathy for the politics in Algiers. "It is to flex the muscle of authority that they do it," he says. He tells me that all over France now there are these flyovers by *La Force de Frappe*.

Does he care? I do not know his politics, but I know that *le patron* is angry about two things being championed by the present government. One is a rule that no child may be taught to read at home, they must all learn at the same time at school so no child will have an advantage. The other is that no one may work more than thirty-five hours. Inspectors have been sent out to issue warnings to workers who exceed the allotted time. He reads about these things and spits.

You seemed to work yourself out of your funk as you went along in your letter. Perhaps your trip to Vermont cleared your head? That would accord with your maxim. I have regaled Obsidienne and Gigi with the account of your giving the run to the bear with yellow claws. As we do not get bears here we can only imagine the smell. O & G join me in applause. About your operation, what can I say? It is most regrettable. I am ashamed to have written about my adventures and passed on that rude joke. Out of his discretion or his guilt Alan did not mention it. It would happen only rarely here. I admire your manly spirit in carrying on.

It is a strange thing, this correspondence. In coming to know yours, my own life has come into sharper focus. I like your looking with the eyes of surprise to see things for me. I am doing the same for you.

For all of us, it is novelty we are after. Here in Cassis the talk is food and weather and fish, *boules*, the outrages of the *Front National* and what is the football. You think this life is exciting? It is boring sometimes. Your life in the books has more variety than mine on the waves and in Cassis where always I see the same ones. My corners never change. Yet in the correspondence it all takes on a novelty, a vividness. As we tell our lives we see its beauties.

There is even beauty in the *boules*. It is a game for men but I am told some women are taking it up. I've not seen them play. Groups of older men, six or ten to a party, gather in the park by the fountain in the afternoon after the hard sun has passed. Each carries his lucky cloth to polish the balls before he pitches. Their special cloths are often in tatters, but they wear nice shoes these men, the older the nicer. The retireds who are too feeble to play sit on the bench and comment. They wear the finest shoes, soft green ones, oranges, reds. Of course they are of a certain class. The Algerians, Tunisians and Moroccans are not so careful about their shoes and do not play in the fountain yard except sometimes in the mornings. They have their regular place on the square with the phone booths.

The beauty in the game is how quietly happy these men are when they play. They concentrate and grow very serious, then they laugh and congratulate each other. Together they are boys again. Just as I have never seen anyone win I have never known anyone to lose. Even the sour old M'sieur Pinet of the Weather Office smiles when he plays. He carries only one ball to the game, but he carries his lucky cloth.

Now and then a group of players will admit a young man to their party. They coach him, they show him the correct postures for the pitches, they teach him to polish the ball. The young man is always quiet and deferential in their company. He does not join them in the yelling and backslapping. But when his hair is gray he will be one of them. He will play when he can imagine his own head as one of those rolling skulls and find amusement in bowling it.

I liked meeting your friends Max and Ike in the correspondence. I'll join Max in his snake game with you. I would join him in barking as you approach his yard and crouch and slither with him as you draw close. Together we would surprise you—but of course our fine tails would give us away!

We have a dog here that walks sideways like Ike. He is a setter. He was hit by a small *camion*—which is our delivery van. I do not know him, but I think he could walk straight if he wanted to. However, since his accident he is always watching over his shoulder for another *camion*.

Most of all I would like to accompany the book van. Alan has found the perfect vehicle for it here, a down-at-heel Citroen panel van leaking its fluids and airs, so it appears to have been abandoned. It would be fine for the camping. Vans for camping we call *caravanes*. I imagine a book run with Alan and Tom in this caravan, hearing the conversations, eating the barbeque and swimming in the lake where it is illegal, dispatching raccoons in the night. What is a skunk?

A change would be a good thing for both of us. So—*Voila*!—you come here and assist with the School for a term, I will come back with Alan and sell the books. Already I know some of your titles: Victor Hugo, Albert Camus, Marcel Proust—these we have in our flat. We have the Hugo in 17 volumes bound in red leather with black and gold stamping, by *Le Club Français Du Livre* we bought on credit and which we are still paying for. It is part of the debt you asked about. We also have Shakespeare in 12 volumes from the same Club and on the same arrangement. You thought I was an ignorant peasant dog? I am surrounded by the ornaments of culture!

Speaking of ornaments, it is a shame that with the American flags of independence no *tricolore* waves from a mast in your town on July 4. We French had almost as much to do with the defeat of the English in your Revolutionary War as the legions from Massachusetts. Say the word and I will commit a flag to *La Poste*. You might incite your Polish neighbors, too, to reflect on their history and display the flag of Poland, for were there not Polish heros of your Revolution?

This month we have had *La Coupe du Monde*—the World Cup of football here. The Team of France has done very well. Last night Croatia went down to us in *le match* 2-1. We were at dinner with a dignified lady who contributes to the handicapped; the roars from Le Golfe, where there is a large television, let us know that things were going well.

To the loudest shouts possible of *"Allez Les Bleus!"*—our team wears blue—free champagne was poured in the restaurant by Patrick, *le patron* of La Vieille Auberge, who presented himself in white pants, a broad sash of carmine, and a deep blue shirt. His cheeks were painted with stripes of red, white and blue—the colors of France. Squads of boys aged 8 to14, painted in the same colors in three long stripes from their toes through their hair, raced up and down the port carrying the *tricolore*. It was merry! We all barked and no one hushed us. *Le patron*'s friend is reserved and aristocratic, but on news of the first goal she opened her capacious purse to pull out one of those compressed air-horn affairs—the kind sailors carry for fog—which she blasted away with joyfully. By game's end her horn was reduced to a little bleat and she was dancing with her hands over her head to North African rhythms. "We all know this," she yelled, "it is in our blood to be Arabs."

Patrice then presented his dancing women with large bunches of lavender to give their dancing a special effect. Of course all the women then swirled with abandon as the men took up the large white table napkins to wave with rhythm as they stepped and turned also. When the victory was clinched a few women bared their breasts to great applause. This is the French custom. The girls do not do this, but their mothers do.

Amidst the bedlam a hundred games broke out on the port, the painted boys leading the charge with long driving runs from Le Golfe to La Caravelle. Balls flew everywhere, the dogs barked and chased, and Jonnie, our tiny waiter who looks to be nine and is really fourteen, put on his shirt with the name of our most famous shooter, Zinedine Zidane, and was out the door like a rabbit, followed closely by the tall drunken Van Dutchman from Freisland who no doubt was a star kicker once—as he'd told us at length—but tonight, with his black stogie glowing, he kicked, missed, and goaled himself into the drink. We got him out OK, but his cigar was a loss.

All night long boys in cars drove around honking horns and waving their flags and shouting , "*Vive La France*! But you must understand, Jefe, this is passion—what we call *engouement*—it is not patriotism. These people would not vote "for France" for anything. With us it is the family first, maybe the village, sometimes the *Département*. Rarely is any issue larger than the family. Is it so different with you?

You have asked about the dog's life here. It is well known that every French family has a dog. We French dogs are indulged like children when we are young. Our people take time with us to teach us how to live in the family, in the café, in the market. We ride on their arms when we are too little to travel on the leash. They teach us our work. How can one take work seriously if he is not raised to it? If you do not take time with the raising of children and the raising of dogs, how will they know what is expected and what to do? Like you, we travel everywhere with our people. But given our training, most of the time we are off leash.

I have never seen anyone strike a dog. I have heard dogs spoken to sharply—the Independents especially, when they are away from their people and commit a rudeness. But generally we are not scolded. It is a great embarrassment to be scolded. That is because of our training. We all know what we are supposed to do.

I have acquaintances in the town, but since I work most of the time and *le patron* keeps me on leash when we are not on our end of the port, I do not have an opportunity to range around with the Independents. Given my class I do not meet the society dogs. My acquaintances all work.

First among them, as you know, because I see her every morning when we walk down to work, is Gigi, the plump gray mastiff who works at Boutique Emmanuel. Her collar is a broad black leather band studded with silver. It goes well with her color and her embonpoint. She is proud to tell you that her breed is *Le Mastif de L' Angleterre*.

These mornings she likes to doze in the doorway—that's where the best sun is. She is an ornament to the pots of clematis and the bunches of sunflowers sold there. Customers have to step over her when they come in. It amuses her when the customers hesitate out of fear. She is of such a placid nature, she is not to be feared, but strangers do not know that. Alan admits that he is hesitant to go in when she is sprawled in the doorway.

I am very fond of her, and now when I have evenings out Gigi pays me some attention. Courtship without attention she says is like cooking but never eating.

When the traffic is diverted she sleeps in the middle of the Avenue Victor Hugo. She knows the hours of the diversions. Sometimes Jean-Marie, the proprietor of the Café Napoléon will come out and make a show of shaking her paw while she is lying down.

Her son, Brummel, is now about also, a bit clumsy and too eager to play to fit well into shop life. He forgets where he is, turns suddenly or jumps in play and the pots go flying. The two of them together outside pester the tourists at Le Bar de la Marine for ends of beer. They fancy it as much as you do! Brummel has put Gigi up to this. The locals do not mind, few of them drink beer anyway.

Another of my particular friends you have also met in the correspondence, the gleaming black Labrador bitch about town—Obsidienne. She is distinguished by an everyday kerchief of fine yellow silk. She tells me she enjoys hearing the music of my work. She too is pleased with my attentions.

And there is Sophie Tucker, the large black Newfoundland who handles the papers and tobaccos at L'Astrée where Alan buys his *Herald Tribune* every morning. With her heavy coat she finds it hot now, so in the early morning, when the men from the town wash down the sidewalks outside her shop, she pesters them for a splash from their thick yellow hoses, and they oblige, nearly knocking her over, but she is pleased and gives a huge shake and retires to her cool spot. The smell of her wet fur mixes curiously with the fragrances of the tobaccos, but no one mentions it.

Usually I am only off leash while we are at work on the port and at sea, but on our return to town I am snapped to the broad red strap, and at home, except for the moments of intimacy, the door to the street is shut to me.

Jean-Michel says I need my rest. It is true. When we get home and I have had my meal I sleep until I hear him stirring at 4:30. I even sleep through the movies, although he plays them very loud. But for the sakes of Gigi and Obsidienne I am learning that I can do with a little less rest.

Among the male dogs in town I like the black Labrador named Whiskey who helps manage the two-star tourist hotel. He wears a gray Hermes silk around his neck and attends the *Réception*. Sometimes he swings into the restaurant. He will accept a morsel from the diners. *Le patron* will not allow me to take anything from a stranger.

Whiskey teased me once for the way I walk. He said I have a staggering gait! But, Jefe, you must understand how that comes from working on a rocking boat. Don't you experience the same thing when you get out of your book van? You're OK aboard, but when first back on steady land you are not agile? It is an odd thing.

Anyway, when Whiskey made that rude observation I invited him to join me for a dive from the lighthouse pier. He has not made that personal remark again.

I exchange greetings with the Belgian shepherd named Sultan who is associated with D'Angelina Pasta e Vino. He is large and graceful with beautiful languid manners. He is pedigreed. I am told that his full name—something much longer than Sultan—is in the computer of pedigreed dogs in Paris. Because he is pedigreed, a long number is tattooed on the inside of his ear. This must have been very painful, but he will not discuss it. I have no tattoo as I have no pedigree.

Sultan used to live in a château above the town. With his master he would frequent Angelina's restaurant every evening. When his master died Sultan moved down and became part of Angelina's family. He glides by the tables. He is too noble to accept handouts but he will allow strangers to pat him.

I do not like strangers to touch me. My ears are sensitive. I allow the children to pat and embrace me, but when Parent's Day comes *le patron* has to tell them to keep their distance. The gentlemen and ladies all want to pet me. They've heard of my teaching and guarding their children and they believe they owe an acknowledgment. I am sent under the desk in *le patron*'s office then, and I am glad to go.

Among my other friends in town, there's an aged shepherd named Lafayette who handles the ladies dress shop Driver on the rue A. Thiers, but he lies down on the job. Not asleep; he takes in all the fashions, but prone and sometimes lying on his side. He believes that he is nineteen years old! It is from him that I get the stories of Jean-Michel's past with the sailing school. He suffers from the "milk eye," the slow clouding over that blinds the old dogs here. They can do nothing for it.

A younger shepherd named Gamine works at the photograph shop on La Rue de la Fontaine. She has a more energetic lying-down pose than Lafayette, all paws-together and ready to leap. We passed her one Market Day. Someone had given her a fine bloody joint. She was enjoying it when an Independent stopped by and expressed interest. Gamine let out a wail of anguish. *Le patron* and I shooed that Independent off. She admires me for my bravery of that day.

Some of the dogs that work the cafés I know slightly. People here select their cafés the way Englishmen select their clubs. *Le patron* meets his friends at Le France or Le Bar de la Marine, depending on the time of day.

Cassis is a noisy town. There are many motorscooters here. One afternoon when *le patron* and I were at Le France a large lady climbed aboard her scooter outside the bakery. She had her bag of vegetables in one hand, her *baguettes* in the other. Two stout dogs stood on opposite sides of her machine barking steadily. She started it up. When the plume of blue smoke appeared they jumped into the little space between her feet, one nose-out to the left, the other nose-out to the right. So you had tails and noses waving out on each side under the market bags as the scooter putted off in its fine cloud.

We ran into her again. She was pulling up to Le Café Manou. Her Vespa was still rolling when the two dogs dropped off like conductors from a slowing train. They proceeded into the café. They work there. They are not young. Their boarding and dismounting is an art.

I intended in my last to tell you about the *fête* of *Le Sacré-Coeur*. It is singular to this region. In May, 1720, the plague hit Marseille. Within a few months 30,000 souls— a third of the town— had perished. The Bishop made a pledge to God that if the town were spared from oblivion, His name would be honored with day of observance.

La peste relented. Now there is a special Mass offered at noon, and offices and the banks close for the *fête*. *Le Maire* makes an address, the Bishop gives a prayer, and then there is the parade. The gays march, there are bands, groups run floats. All this takes place down La Canebière—the fine long boulevard of Marseille.

The best part of the *fête* is the gays' dancing the *can-can*. Everywhere there is music, so they strut and parade and dance all at the same time in fantastic costumes. Now and then a dancer will swing out of line and take a partner from among the watchers. Sometime the watcher is terrified and scurries away, but usually they are young men and they are glad to dance.

The paraders do this for the remission of AIDS. Some in sequins dance on stilts. This is a great specialty. The men dress like women and you cannot tell. Perhaps some of the women dress like men also, but there are not many women in the parade. Gays from the whole southeast of France gather for this fête. People come from as far away as Aix and Arles to watch them. At the end of the parade there are costume balls that last all night. Everyone is welcome for a contribution. Large sums are raised.

I had to ask *le patron* for help with your riddle. We have no cows here and I know of only one horse. What would be pasture if there were water is vineyard since there is not. We do not even have goats.

My Little Chief, I must close now. The afternoon class starts soon. Keep cheerful! And send another maxim.

Your Friend Rodeo

FAX

August 8, 4 PM

Ben—

Our car was broken into this morning, Mom's purse stolen and my pack. Please cancel the bank and credit cards and FEDEX us replacements.

M's dark glasses went, her address book, her precious folder of family photographs, the keys to the apartment, some letters ready for mailing, your Swiss Army knife, and the two fine melons, fresh loaf, bottle of red wine and kilo of a fine old cheese for a picnic with a friend. Not that we've been hungry. We've been too busy scrambling.

We were out painting, not at our usual place but up in the hills. We'd gone up to escape a shower. We were working fifty feet away. Never heard them. They hit us for our Paris license plates—the mark of a rented car. A quick shot to the door with a hammer and screwdriver and it opened like a shucked oyster. They scooped out the works.

We reported it to the *Gendarmerie*. The young officer in his immaculate uniform sat down at an old typewriter and carefully laid in pink, yellow and green forms with a carbon between each. First question: my date of birth. Next: my mother's maiden name. After an hour of this and not one question about suspects or what exactly was taken he rolled out the forms and stamped each one. We were given a copy and a *bonjour* and, so far as he was concerned, the case was closed.

Dad

August 8, Cassis

Dear Jefe—

I have not heard from you for more than a month—cat got your tongue?

Things jog along here pretty much the same. It is hot, 32° C, which is 94° F for you. By ten in the morning there is a wonderful humming in the woods from the *cigales*—our tree crickets. Do you get them? The locals love them. They bring luck. Every shop for postcards has an array of ceramic ones for sale, some as small as your toe, others as large as cigars. The insect itself is drab and small, hard to see. The ceramic ones are dark green daubed on cream with yellow touches and the wings painted gold. Why are they lucky? Because they are so noisy, yet you can't see them? At some time in the correspondence you must address luck.

Because it is the season of *cigales* the wrens who eat them are happy and sing loudly, though they are no match for the gray doves who cannot stop singing. I think the doves sing so steadily because they always have a lot of food in the kernels of the pine cones.

It is hot now for both of us. Alan tells me Ben gave you a clip, but as he is not expert at manipulating the machine, you got nicks and your coat is ragged. He did not attempt your tail, which may be a good thing. Here, no one would think of clipping his poodle at home—everyone goes to *Le Toilettage*. I shed, so it is not a problem for me, and I can go into the water for my bath at any time.

Le patron wears a white hat these days. The morning class starts at 8, the afternoon at 4:30, to escape the hardest sun. It can get up to 40° C with us now.

I understand your anxiety about thunder. In this hot season we get electric storms with thunders. I do not like them, but I do not go under the bed. I flatten when the great noise comes. I can hear these storms coming before Jean-Michel suspects them. I bark a special warning then.

The electric storms are a peril to sailors. *Le patron* watches the sky when we are out on the water. He brings the class to port when he sees the clouds that bring them.

Do you get storms of wind? At this season *le mistral* comes, a heavy gusting wind off the land. It can blow for days making the doors and windows rattle and sometimes moan like living things. Many dogs howl then. I do not like *le mistral*, but I do not howl.

Strange, for all that it is a storm, when *le mistral* blows it is clear. It is called the storm with blue sky, but we do not go out on the water. It is a windstorm with the sun shining. It brings on cool days.

Perhaps there is a move coming for you? Alan mentions leaving the cold of Massachusetts and relocating by the sea. That way he could continue to swim every day and Martha could keep working outside. But they worry about leaving their friends. The problem is, their friends are not all in one place.

Alan says that in America it is customary for a family to move every seven years. I told him, "If a French family made so many moves it would be thought that they are escaping from something shameful."

"With us it is to start a new life," he replied. "There's not so much looking back in America as looking West. The stories of many families can be traced from the East Coast ports two hundred miles west each generation. Then they hit the Pacific and they double back."

Since I mention them so often and they are so much of our life here, you and the American Gang should know about the dogs we call Independents. I wonder if you have any like them? They are not a pack and they are not related.

Most are male. The Independents in town I know but slightly. They are the dogs who come down in the afternoon from the big houses up in the hills and run free. For all that they are fed at home they cruise the cafés and the *poubelles*—our rubbish bins. They are not serious the way we are. They have no work and no discipline.

I envy them their pleasures with their girlfriends but that is all I envy them. *Le patron* says that because they have no work the Independents make trouble. They can be reckless barkers and careless about where they do things. I bark to warn them away from our end of the port.

They are not pedigreed. They are a unique Provençal mix—the size and gait of a German wirehair pointer; muzzle, head, and coat of a shepherd with some long silky gray mixed in. The colors of their coats are mixed. They have large feet and are distinguished by their rough and rumpled appearance. They are kept to bark at strangers in the night. The Gang of Independents cruising today include Kouqui, Dempsy, Lulu, Gringo, Velours, Louie, and Tutu.

Some claim to be part border collie. People here credit their dogs with Scottish border collie blood the way they credit themselves with forebears from the Bourbons and the Bonapartes. "By way of Adam and Eve," *le patron* says when he hears these claims.

At Presqu'île Martha encountered the border collie named Adagio this morning. His family is responsible for the patrol of the park. His coat is silver and bronze and he wears a brass bell which makes him clank like a goat as he goes around town. He pretends not to hear his bell, but that thing is an embarrassment. He goes like a leper with his warning, and he must be hot in his matted coat. He's fragrant even by my standards, for he does not bathe and he is not delivered to *Le Toilettage*.

Martha said "Well, hello!" as he trotted by to the rhythm of his own band.

He stopped, sniffed, wagged, and peed on her rock.

"Who could ask for more of a greeting?" she said.

She did not understand his message.

Le patron visited at Le France with a man who got to talking about the Independents of Cassis. *Le patron*'s friend said that they are not supposed to run free, but of course they do. Many people on the port like them for their flaunting ways, so when the dogcatcher's little *camion* is spotted coming over the mountain to the port, the "Arab radio" alerts the café owners and they rush to shelter the Independents inside the cafes. When the dogcatcher arrives there are no strays to pick up.

On Sundays it is the fashion for the Independent to wear a bit of cloth around his neck to give him style. Something in lavender or crimson is popular. *Le patron* says that we are workers so we do not dress up like that. Frankly, I'd like a touch of ribbon sometimes. Whiskey wears a quite beautiful bit of gray to show his coat to advantage. I would like to highlight my fine coat. I tell Jean-Michel that a silk of black would be nice. It would set off my ears. He says black is for funerals.

The society dogs I do not know. They visit the cafés with their people. They rarely come out to the far side of the port where I work. It is too rough for them here—the boatyard where the hulls are sanded and repaired, the ship chandler's, the shop for the engines. The noise of the children. This is a rough and yelling place. They could not manage it.

I am as aloof to them as they are to me. Not that they are rude. They are very polite. They do not bark or pee where they shouldn't. When I say aloof, I mean only that they do not notice me. Many are poodles. Some of them do not seem to know that they are dogs, they think they are people.

They sit under the tables or in a lap. The small gray poodle of M'sieur Papazian the ice cream merchant attends his master at his regular table outside Le Bar du XXième Siècle sitting on his man's huge belly. When M'sieur Papazian dozes in his chair his companion rides the belly like a small boat taking swells. It is a surprising thing to see the two of them on the scooter together, both driving! It is curious, I have never seen a fat poodle.

The society dogs are trained to their life. They learn their café manners when they are puppies held in their owners' laps at the café tables. There are always one or two in training at Le France on a sunny morning. They are comfortable in cars. Many of the smaller ones ride on the driver's lap, paws on the outside window. The small ones travel to market in an open basket.

But what is their work, I wonder? Perhaps it is enough that they give comfort to their people? Some, of course, are spies for the gypsy gamblers. I have told you about those.

But to have no work? That I would find a hard thing. It is the question of work that troubles Alan. He is not sure what his work is now. He has things he does, but nothing he must do, so what is his vocation? Perhaps the hardest work of all is that which you put yourself to with no obligation and at nobody's telling.

A reporter for *Livre Bleu* asked *le patron* the other day, "Why do you do this work? What do you get out of it?"

He answered, "Our work is what makes us what we are."

Le patron and Alan chewed that over for a long time over coffees. "It is not just the money," they agreed. "The proverb, 'Work is hard, no work is harder' is not just about money. It is about face and self-regard and the excitement of mixing with others. There is no music in idleness. It is at our work that we sing to each other, tell our stories. It is when we work that we are most alive. Work is a gift, not a burden. To have a task, to be needed to do something, that is a blessing and a salvation." That is *le patron*'s view.

Alan compared work to a seed that needs soil to press it down if it is to grow. "So a man needs work to become himself. Work gives order to time; without work time stands still, formless."

Too bad you do not know to eat fish. It is very good here and cheap, but then you live a great distance from the sea. Myself, I prefer ham. When we go to the butcher M'sieur Prevot always has something for me. Is it true what Alan says, that by law you are not allowed to visit in the markets? We dogs of Provence all visit in the shops where our people buy. It is appropriate and expected that the merchant will make a gift to the family dog.

With the Independents it is different. They visit the shops on their own and are not shy with their importunings. Each has his route. One I know, Joe Louis, shows up at Le Marché U at the same time every day to collect the rinds of cheese they save for him.

Tell me, my dancing black friend, do you have a Saint in your town? Here we have Saint Pierre, the patron saint of the *pêcheurs*. The English call him Saint Peter and his fish the John Dory. I don't know what the American for him is. His figure occupies a niche on the passageway Quai Barthélemy.

In his statue he is as big as I am. At night he holds a light to beckon the sailors home. We have a town *fête* to honor him the last Sunday in June. To get ready, all the *pêcheurs* clean and paint their boats. On the evening of the *Fête de Saint Pierre* they circle the inner port in their boats to display their flags and festoons. The Mayor gives a speech and the Priest blesses the fleet. All the lights on the port are illuminated and there is patriotic music from the loudspeakers.

In the morning of his *fête* day the Saint is paraded through the streets on a litter and carried to the port. The fine white cruiser of the *calanques* tours is hung with white flags, Saint Pierre is piped aboard, and he makes a tour of the *Baie*. Every craft that is seaworthy and many that are not join in his parade. They all blow their sea horns. The din is wonderful! You know it is a joyful noise.

That night the children put on their Provençal costumes and dance and sing the old songs to flutes and tambourines. Then there is jousting. Two fishing boats are specially painted with stripes and fitted with long prows and high poops. Strong boys who have trained for it for weeks are armed with poles and dressed in colors to match their boats. The boats push off. The boys fight to push each other into the sea. The winner must make five dunks, but as the one falling off usually pulls his opponent down with him, the joust can last for hours. Long before it is over the announcer has grown tired and the wine has run out.

Do you have a Saint Day *fête* in your town?

It is surprising how many sounds we have here. I cannot imagine the silence Alan says you have in Hatfield. Here there is always the sound of the water, the magpies, the gulls, the wrens, the children, motors, the wonderful *cigales*, doves—all the voices. Take any one of them away and a great hole would be torn in the fabric of our life. The gulls especially—for all I despise them—give a wonderful music to the day when they do not cry like cats. They start early with their high-pitched *ça va*? like the cleaning women on their way to work. That is our first music of the day.

The English joke that the French pay too much attention to food. How can one pay too much attention to food? Not enough food and eventually there are wars and revolutions. Some who were around for the War have the memory of not enough food, and if you go back in history to the starving times you are reminded to eat when you can. I told Alan the saying in this region, "Never pass up a free dinner."

He was going to go out sailing with us this morning. He showed up at 9, but as it was raining he said he would like to try another day. We said OK, but of course we go out every day unless there is a heavy storm. This was not a heavy storm. I do not mind the rain. A & M were off to a hill town where perhaps it would not be raining.

Regards to Maximum, from
Rodeo

August 22, Cassis

Dear Ben,

Thanks for all your help and the telephoning around. We've recovered from the break-in. M's found a replacement purse in the market handsomer than the one she lost and put herself in a better way so far as powders and perfumes are concerned too. But there's no replacing her little book of family pictures and personal notes and favorite postcards.

Hip bothersome. I feel like Mr. Bramble in *Humphry Clinker*, "an odd kind of humorist, always on the fret, and so unpleasant in his manner, that rather than be obliged to keep him company, I'd resign all claim to the inheritance of his estate—Indeed his being tortured by the gout may have soured his temper..."

Our landlord's son is a doctor. He specializes in knees and just wrote an article for a conference in San Francisco. He asked me to go over his English. In exchange I asked him to go over my *hanche*. He was brisk and certain in his twisting. Common arthritis. He gave me some new exercises, said to swim more and go easy on the cuisine.

The paintings come. The apartment is filled with them and the place smells like a pine woods for all the turpentine. Panic when our landlord knocks at the door—what would he make of all this stuff spread about? We're careful, but wet paint travels.

This is the hot season. It is 94 degrees on our porch at 2 PM. The water is perfect. I go swimming at 7 in the morning and again in the evening. Most afternoons we nap from 2-3 in the dark part of our flat with a noisy fan going to make us think of a storm in Vermont.

Jean-Michel has given me his dossier, an inch-thick collection of magazine and newspaper interviews, letters from students, photographs—one of him when he was 20—a tough!—a letter from l'Abbé Simon saying that Mon. Beaujon is qualified to teach diving, a picture of the two of them together, father and son.

The sailing and swimming school is only a part of his work. He also teaches diving, but I don't know when he does that. There's a lot in the dossier about his work for the *incapacitateds* and quotes from interviews:

"I confirm their faith. I teach them how to become masters of themselves. Before twelve they are weak. Anyone can control them. That is why the young make such good soldiers—they prefer certainty over questions, the uncertainty of life threatens them. Boys of twelve make the best fanatics. This I saw in the war. They did not care about dying, they cared about the rules of the cult."

"They learn to impose a discipline upon themselves. As they learn to manage their own body they come to see how strong the discipline is, the muscle and control it builds."

"I coach each one for technique. At the same time I help him search out his path. I've had one, a girl, who has gone planting trees with the *Garde Forestier*; for another it is tending to his grandfather.

"I explain that when I am on my path I am strong. When I am not on my path I am tempted. 'Do not deceive yourself,' I tell them, 'violence comes with many faces.'"

I asked our landlord if he knew Jean-Michel.

"I know who he is, but we are not acquainted. There are so many strange names around now. Everything is getting mixed together."

"Like America?"

"You never had a tradition. We had a tradition. Now there are foreign names on the mailbox downstairs!"

I let it go. We had tea. English tea from Fortnum and Mason, served with a tin of English biscuits. Even the china was English, and the small spoons. This is extraordinary. Everything in this country is French—the garlic press, the olive oil, the cars, the appliances. To the French, only French goods have quality. Except in the matter of afternoon tea.

I looked over the mailbox names: Clauzet, Marchetti, Nicolas, Mazel, Melay, Rodange, Ducroux. Not a Hatfield list.

We were invited for *apéritifs* by Henri, the man I thought I'd offended by asking if he'd been in the *Résistance*. For all he seemed a little shy about it before, tonight he told us more stories about the War here.

He was 20 when the Germans invaded France. He was in the French Navy, deserted at Marseille when the French merchant seamen were ordered to become part of the German merchant marine.

He hid out in Marseille. Because he was a deserter and had no papers, he took an ill-paid draftsman's job in a plant being built to make synthetic oil. He had to make do without ration stamps or any benefits. He lived on fish, rutabagas and "black turnips."

"Many starved here. This is not a food-growing region, just vines. But I could spear fish from the rocks. I survived on fish. I do not like to eat fish any more. Now I eat beef and pork and sausage and cheese at every opportunity! And omelettes!"

He was not laughing.

"The local authorities were looking for me. Police were posted at the train and bus stations. So I had to travel on foot at night. I could not have taken the bus from Marseille to Cassis even if I'd had the money.

"All the men between 17 and 55 were required to register. Many were sent to the labor camps in Germany. Those who remained had to take turns guarding the railroad from guerilla attacks. If a section was blown up, the guards on duty were shot. The local gendarmes knew I was around, but I never signed up. They'd come to my mother's flat asking for me, but I was never at home there."

"Were you ever afraid?" Martha wanted to know.

"Scared, yes. Afraid, no. We were young."

Suddenly he jumped up exclaiming, "My God! There will be a fire!"

He rushed into his kitchen and returned with a plate heaped with hot puff pastries stuffed variously with bits of meat, sausage, cheese, tomatoes, anchovies. A half hour later he produced another, and an hour after that a large dish of sweets. We were not invited for dinner. This meal which is not a meal and precludes eating a meal is called *apéritif*.

During the War his mother had an apartment in Cassis. Every week Henri would walk a trail over the hills from Marseille—20 miles—to stay with her, cadge a meal, and see his buddies in town.

"I knew all the paths. I ran like a goat. I could do it in less than four hours."

They frequented two cafés which were frequented by German Navy officers. The officers wore heavy black belts with daggers which they hung over the coatrack when they settled at their tables.

One evening Henri and his pals swaggered in with ropes around their waists with bicycle pumps attached. These they hung on the coatracks with much fanfare. The Germans just laughed. "The Navy, they were not Nazis," Henri said.

Not so funny a while later when a friend and he were caught in the streets at midnight. Curfew was 9P.M. They'd been out dancing. They ran for it, one to the left, the other to the right. His friend got caught, spent the night in jail cleaning the Germans' boots. Henri said that if he'd been caught and made to do that he would have shot the officer whose boots he had to clean.

"You carried a gun?" Martha asked.

"Oh no, you were shot on the spot if they caught you with a weapon. But I had a gun. And I would have found him and I would have shot him."

I asked if the underground was active here.

"No, no place to hide. No forests. But there was sabotage, yes. At our synthetic oil plant we never produced a drop. Every time we got ready to start it up a turbine would fail or there would be a problem with the boiler."

He had another Scotch and told us that after he'd deserted from the merchant fleet he teamed up with a friend named Dupuy. Together they fitted out a small boat they'd found abandoned at Port

Miou to make for Gibraltar. They worked eight months fixing the engine and lining up fuel. They were about ready to go in November, 1942. On the 11th the Germans occupied the south of France and set up machine guns around the port. No way to get out.

Dupuy was a couple of years older. He'd been an officer in the French Army, jailed in Germany for guerilla activities. He escaped with a girl, killing two guards. The Germans had published a "Wanted" poster with his picture. Dupuy kept a copy pasted on the wall of his Cassis apartment.

"Before you deserted," I said, "when you were in the merchant fleet, did your ship call in neutral ports? Why didn't you go over to the English?"

"The English!" he spat. "They sank our fleet at Oran. We were given six hours to surrender, but we had no steam! We could not move. They sank eight of our fifteen warships there. They said they did it to keep the ships from going to the Nazis, but our admirals would never have allowed that. Fifty-five hundred of our sailors perished. We hated the English for that.

"Then we did not know what the Germans were doing to the North, but we knew what the English had done here!"

I asked him about the plaque for the Free French submarine. He just shrugged. "There were many sinkings."

I was going to ask him why he didn't join the Free French Navy, but I let it go. He'd said as much as he wanted to tonight. The clam is opening.

The key is his pal Dupuy. Dupuy scouted the coast and collected information about the shore guns between Marseille and Cassis. He knew when the submarines were coming. Is Dupuy still alive?

But maybe Henri is the key. He speaks German. One of Ellen's guides spoke German.

I inquired at *La Mairie* and *Le Bureau du Tourisme* about the war monuments. No one can tell me about the submariners of December, 1943, or the ship's mission. As for the *Résistance*, there are no records, and anyway the *maquis* were communists, and that was bad too. And Vichy? Vichy at least was French. Pétain was a great man. Vichy was a buffer between Germany and Spain. It would have been worse here without Vichy.

What does it come to? Some German Navy came here for R&R. There was wine in the cafés and fish in the sea. There are facts of life and there are politics. The facts here in Cassis were not so bad, so perhaps there were no politics, or what politics there were were for the easier way, no confrontation.

The War is becoming my business. The plaques, the traces of fortifications which the trees and plants are softening and taking over—was this part of Ellen's life? I was four when she came to us but I can still see her haunted face. Was she part of this place?

"You bombed here," our landlord tells us, "American and British planes came over bombing." Not here exactly, but at Marseille. One Saturday morning at 11 A.M. 200 Allied bombers hit Marseille. The old locals remember that. "The sky was black with your planes."

It was all clearer before I got here: the French against the Germans, for the English, for the Americans. But there is no "French." There are those of the north, the southeast, the west, the monarchists, the communists, the socialists, Free French, Vichy, pro-Revolution, anti-, those who regret Napoléon, those who adore him. It all swirls together like the colors of the sea, bands of blue to greens to dark and the ripples fluttering here and there, some blown this way, some that—and this is a calm day! How to make sense of it?

What does it have to do with Vietnam? What does it have to do with me? Everything and nothing.

We hung around the port until 11 last night listening to a Peruvian string-and-flute band as it gigged along past all the good restaurants. Poignant, that stuff! "Ours," Martha said, "American."

Overheard: "The Jews and the Arabs are the interesting ones. They have all the history."

Hug yourself and the Jefe dog for me.

Dad

FAX

August 23

Ben—

Case not closed. The Mariner turns out to be a detective dog. The Police are impressed.

Yesterday afternoon as he and Jean-Michel passed the boatyard, Rodeo noticed some boys in the corner. They weren't familiars. He smelled something curious. He smelled my pack—the residue of all those beef kidney treats. He'd heard about our *fracture*. Bang! he put it all together.

He rushed the boys. J-M was close behind, calling him back. Then he noticed the knapsack and it all clicked with him too.

Rodeo guarded the three boys—19, 20, 23, all locals—while J-M summoned the Police.

Their van was searched. There was stuff from other raids. They'd ditched Mom's purse, our letters, the glasses. Recovered: pack, Swiss Army knife, cosmetics and camera. Sold: my books for the price of a beer.

Our apartment keys were sold along with the credit and bank cards. Good that you'd canceled the plastic. We'd changed the locks.

The Police were most curious to know who they'd sold the keys and plastic to. The owner of the van. He has a ring.

Of the 6000FF the boys were caught with (about $1,000), we got 2,000, which we wanted to give Rodeo as his reward. J-M was diffident about accepting, but at the mention of his name Rodeo's delicate ears flicked ever so slightly and he cocked his head. J-M got the signal. The francs went into his trunks.

Dad

August 23, Cassis

Hey Jefe—

Another long silence from you! What's up?

If you envied me before, envy me more now! Tonight I am proud, rich and famous, and I have a dossier with the Police! Have I committed some crime, some robbery, and been apprehended with guns and sirens in the company of a beautiful woman like one of your *Miami Vice* boys?

No. I did an "Ah Ha!" like Sherlock Holmes, a "*Voila*!" like Mon. Poirot, a "Gotcha!" like the L.A. cop on TV.

You have heard about the robbery? I noticed right away when Alan came around that he was not wearing his *sac a dos*. Break-ins are common here. With so much unemployment gangs of young men and women seek out the rented cars. Tourists are likely to be traveling with valuable baggages.

This evening we left the School late. We were tired and hungry. We had conducted the classes and repaired a tiller. It was quiet in our quarter, the time of going to the cafés for *apéritifs*. No lovers had come to nestle against our wall, no fishermen had set up on the lighthouse pier.

As we passed the boatyard I heard whispering and smelled the sweet drug. Three toughs were huddled in the far corner. Then I smelled beef kidney! There was the the red *sac*! I raced to find my treat.

Le patron followed. Right away he knew they were the thieves. He looked at each one long and carefully. To one he said, "I know you. You live on *la rue* such-and-such." To another, he said, " I have seen you on the motorcycle of Jules Lamont." The third he studied the longest. "I do not know you, but I have memorized your face. I leave the dog to guard you. Injure him and I will kill you one by one; but it is likelier that he will injure you if you so much as move."

The big toughs I saw huddled over their cigarette of *la drogue* shrank to little boys when *le patron* addressed them. He went back to our *bureau* to call the Police.

Among themselves they swore to admit nothing. They would say they'd found it all.

The Police came and stripped them and looked at them. Every item they had was gone over, every piece of identification, all their keys. One set of keys excited curiosity. One of the Police left with the keys. He came back a few minutes later. He had located their caravan with booty from other break-ins.

A & M were called. They identified their things and gave a statement.

The boys had some money. The Police said that it must have been stolen also and gave A & M a share. They handed it to *le patron* for me. I see another beef kidney coming. Tonight I am the richest dog in Cassis, and well praised.

Regards. If you have any mysteries that need untangling, e-mail me: "Sleuth@Cassis."

Rodeo

Labor Day, September 4, Hatfield

Sleuth@Cassis—

Good work! You must be rolling in beef kidneys. With G & O and the Independents you are playing *boules* with them in the square reserved for the aristocrats!

I haven't written because since I complained about being left behind, Ben has taken me on his trips to New York, we've done the book van in Vermont, and gone to see Aunt Margie to ask about the War. And to keep fit Ben is doing longer and longer bike rides. He cruises around looking for tag sales. He goes over house stuff like a bird collecting for a nest. Something is up with him.

We set out before seven in the morning and often don't make it back until lunchtime. Since I can't doze on the bicycle I'm losing a lot of sleep which I have to make up.

We've had the tobacco harvest. With flashing hatchets the black men from Jamaica chopped the plants off at the ground. The family whose field it is works behind the cutters, gathering the heavy tops and hooking them to long drying poles on rolling racks. Each field must be cut when it is dry, and no rain can fall on the cut top or it will rot, so all the workers work fast with their eyes on the sky. The racks of tobacco are rushed to the barns with many doors for drying. Our roads are filled with slow parades of rolling racks drawn by every tractor that has a wheeze left in it.

The potato farmers have sprayed their fields with a chemical to make the plant think that frost has struck and it should stop growing. The green turns brown overnight. They do this so the root will not grow large and soft. A machine comes and digs the potatoes and dumps them into V-bottomed trucks. Those trucks weave among the tobacco tractors on their way to the potato storage, which must be cool and dark. Along the roads now you can pick up all you need of tobacco and potatoes.

Szawlowski is our czar of potatoes because he has the storage. You have your czar of ice cream on the port? We have our czar of potatoes on the river! Personally, I prefer ice cream.

Today is a holiday. The union leaders march, our President gives a speech about how good wages are and says the economy is booming, everybody who wants to be President gives a speech saying that wages are lousy and the economy is crashing. For some it booms, for some it crashes. Ben says it used to be the job of government to even things out so that no one crashed, but we don't hear that in the speeches now. On the big highways the cars are sleek; on the side streets of New York where he has his apartment, people who look like they haven't washed for days ask for money. Does our government even keep score any more? What is the economy like with you? Is Socialism fairer?

On the unbuttoned dilemma of our President, Sandy at The Dairy Mart said to Ben this morning: "I like Clinton, I love him, but he gives philanthropy a bad name."

Over the weekend Ben and I set up Zora with Tom in Brattleboro and did $120. Tom held court. His friends stopped to visit on their way home from the Farmer's Market. As their lettuces wilted Tom declaimed some poems he likes by Walter de la Mare: "In the water clear as air/ Lurks the lobster in his lair," and a strange one that goes, "Twinkum, twankum, twirlum, twitch—/My great grandam—She was a Witch. . ." We spent the night at Tom's, which leads me to explain another cause of my long silence. A cat did get my tongue, the cat who caused my injury.

When Abby moved to California she couldn't take her cat Miste along, and sure as hell that cat couldn't come live with us.

Tom likes cats. He has a large one named Koli whose prior owners had him declawed, so Koli is afraid to go outside because he can't protect himself. Tom thought that if Miste would come and live with them, perhaps she'd protect Koli.

They gave it a try. At first there was no friendship between them, but gradually things got to the

point where Tom would put them both outside and close the door.

Koli was afraid. Miste immediately picked up on that, and why. When Koli was out Miste would hang around. If a neighbor's dog approached, Miste took him on. She likes a fight. Koli had found his protector.

Soon they were to be found dozing together on the kitchen table, although Miste kept several hideouts on the shelves behind Tom's books and on one radiator that had been forgotten for all the furniture piled around.

Tom's house is a wonder. There is confusion there for everyone except Tom, his wife Mary, and the cats. It holds the furniture and papers of everyone in the family since the first Cabots and Holbrooks walked out from Boston and set up there before the Revolution.

So Miste settled in with Koli and Tom. She settled in with Mary too, but Mary sort of floats above everything and doesn't pay much attention to the cats. Or to Tom for that matter. Not that she's unfriendly, she's just one of those very slender women who's always somewhere else, and even she cannot tell you where that is.

When Alan would pick up Tom for a book van run, I'd go in the house. The cats would hide of course, and I'd finish off their tuna and cream and the piles of dried cat food. Tom is one for food! He always puts out more than they can eat, which is OK for Miste, she stays thin, but not good for Koli. He gets larger and larger. Soon Tom will have to hoist him up to the bed. Already Tom has set up a box as a sort of mounting stage, and Koli can barely clear that with his belly.

So. I've written you about Ben's important new friend. A few weeks ago Ben brought her to Vermont to meet Tom and Mary. They all got along, so Tom offered to make the dinner of Reggio Calabria that his mother used to make. There was a bottle of Chianti, then another.

Before the first bottle was half gone I'd eaten all the food. I went exploring. Koli was installed on Tom's bed like the king of the mountain. He acknowledged me, I acknowledged him. It didn't occur to me to chase him, and he realized that. The truth is, these days I'm finding it harder and harder to jump.

"I suppose you are looking for your friend," Koli said.

I was stunned.

" 'Friend'? Do you mean Miste?"

Then I thought, Why not? Our war was fought years ago. So much had changed.

"She's behind *The Arabian Nights*."

It took a while, but I found *The Arabian Nights*. Sixteen volumes, and they weren't under "A." Miste had a whole apartment back there.

"Hello Miste," I called.

A stirring. And then, amazing! A purr.

"Hello Jefe."

"Long time."

"Long time."

"How are you? How's life here?"

"OK. Life here's OK. I miss Abby and her friends. You didn't know them, but they used to tell their dreams of life to each other for hours and hours. It was like music. Their voices together were like music. It was pretty to hear.

"It's quiet here. Tom and Mary don't say much. Mary's away a lot. Tom plays movies, but the voices of movies don't make the music of conversation.

"And Tom speaks mainly to Koli. They are companions. Koli sleeps on the bed. I do not. Tom and I exchange pleasantries, but talk? No. We do not talk. He picks me up by my middle and rubs my head sometimes. He has big stubby hands. He is not gentle. Only Abby and Martha know how to pick me up. I love it when Martha comes to visit. She always picks me up.

"The deal is, I board here, I watch out for Koli. The food is good, the house is warm. But I'm a little bit lonely. Life was best with Abby.

"How about with you?"

She peeped out over vol. 7. She was safe. I couldn't reach her. I didn't want to. I told her about A & M being away, my living with Ben, his head in the book he's writing and his heart in New York.

"I'm lonely too. I sleep a lot."

"Me too. The girl he's with, she's good for him," Miste said. "They laugh together. They look something alike, strong and blond. They'll grow old looking more and more alike. That's good in a couple. We always look for something of ourself in the other. A mirror. It's best if the mirror gives back something of the original."

A long silence. Then I told her the story of the fall afternoon she and I rode to college together with Ben and Alan to deliver Abby's stuff.

"They had us in the pet carriers. It was raining. I'd had to get out for a duty. I got wet and muddy. The wet, the warm, the close air—it was fragrant in that car.

"Alan was driving. The one-way streets, the drizzle—suddenly he was heading down the wrong way. A car was trying to turn in. Alan tried to turn around. Couldn't. Honks. Two black guys on the sidewalk were lugging a refrigerator. They looked over and laughed. Over the horns and barking, one called to the other, 'Somebody oughta teach that mother how to drive!'

"We got to Abby's room. Her roommate's mom was there. She'd just laid down a nice white rug. I forgot about my muddy paws, I just wanted to roll in that rug and dry off."

Miste stretched and purred. She came down. The dinner of Reggio Calabria went on and on. We storied each other for hours and we didn't feel lonely any more. Koli listened and smiled.

At last it was time to go up the long hill to the cabin. I stood by the door. Miste was on the kitchen table.

Tom knew.

"Friends now, huh?"

So I have a new friend out of an old enemy. She knows my worst and I know hers, so we are worn in together like an old suit, and nothing between us catches or pulls. When we go to Tom's now I have something to look forward to besides scarfing the cream and tuna.

You know, I exaggerated a little when I told you I'd bitten off her tail. Maybe I got a mouthful of fur, but I didn't get the whole tail. She still has it.

A large map of Europe is spread out on the dining table here. Ben and Margie drew a red line showing the escape route the person from our family followed out of Germany fifty-five years ago. There is an "X" for every stop Margie remembers hearing about. The escapers went down rivers. The final "X" is near you, at Marseille.

It's late. We're going to New York to take Ben's girl home. When we visit she locks her cats in the kitchen. They are terrified of me, which is gratifying.

Goodnight from Hatfield with this from Pascal: "Had Cleopatra's nose been shorter, the whole face of the earth would have changed."

Jefe

PS—Ben just read in the *Times* that the French are afflicted with "*la morosité*." What is this? Are you morose?

September 15, Cassis

Jefe *le chien,* my brave American—

OK that you had a reunion with the cat of your youth. The ones we share a history with are the ones who remind us who we were. Sometimes this is unpleasant, but mostly it is a good thing as it keeps us to our true path. Best of all, with the old friends we are not lonely; with new friends, often, we are. There can be long silences in a conversation with an old friend; with a new friend a silence is an embarrassment. But what a strange name that cat has. Miste? What does *Miste* mean?

At last your patron went out on the sea with us!

We let him help with the preparations. We took him into the tackle room and fitted him with an orange life vest from the long racks where they hang to dry. Then he went with the children into the room where the masts, sails and tillers are kept. He admired the order of it all, every mast and sail numbered and stepped in its assigned place, every keel and tiller numbered to its corresponding boat and ranked in order.

Alan is beginning to appreciate how much care and order we must teach the children before we even get to the water! He admired very much the organization of our school.

He wore his hat against the sun and cheered the children as they maneuvered among the buoys.

This was a class of advanced students, so when the wind picked up *le patron* declared a race. We all yelled *"Allez! Allez! Allez!"* as hard as we could. *Le patron* raised his fist and shouted "*Giddyup Ongawa*!" to his little sailors. When one executed a good maneuver he yelled "Ho! Ho! Ho!" For all he is a tough coach to the little ones, *le patron* is generous in his praise. Always at the end of the race he will pat each head and say, “Super!” or “Well fought!”

But I do not think Alan enjoyed it. Today there were swells and *Zodiac* bobbed and heaved. The sea was not really heavy, but perhaps there were traces of *le blanc bleu*—what you call whitecaps. Your patron grew quiet.

I allowed him to pet me when he grew uneasy.

To my surprise he asked *le patron* if I was trembling because I was cold.

“No,” said Jean-Michel. “Rodeo does not get cold.”

He explained that I am tense because I must always be ready to jump into the water and perform a rescue. I must watch every boat and listen to the children to detect an urgency.

“And you are also poised in readiness to catch a seagull, yes Rodeo?”

When people ask him why I bark so much it is his joke to tell them that I am annoyed with the seagulls. He jokes that I bark to drive off the seagulls. In fact I do not care a fig about seagulls. True, I like their music sometimes, but sometimes when they cry they sound like cats and then they annoy me. But I have never even snapped at a seagull. They are too unimportant to bother with.

After class *le patron* and I walked to the fish shop together. Marie was there dozing on her bench. They talked about the problem with old Lucienne, the *fadade* who sings for tips at the café tables and accosts strangers for money. Marie must watch out for Lucienne. They are related by marriage. Marie has the responsibility of her. Lucienne is tiny. She is rich with properties. She is crazy because she is afraid she will be poor. *Le patron* said that we are all poor and naked but for our faith. He says that is what he learned from l’Abbé Simon.

He tells the children of the Sailing School a story he got from L’Abbé. A boy was offered an orange by a priest who asked him to say where God is. The boy replied, “Please sir, tell me first where God is not?”

“Lucienne is poor in faith,” *le patron* explained as we walked home. “She is very regular to go to

Mass, but she does not believe it is protection enough. That is her poverty. That is why she is afraid and walks on the port all night asking for money. The old hawk is hunched over by her fear of being without money."

Last week Jean-Michel took the fast train to Paris to do an exhibition dive. He does this every year from a height of 30 meters, which for you would be the height of a 4-story building. They close one of the bridges near Notre Dame and build a scaffold for the dive. It is well-publicized. He does this to buy artificials for people who have lost a limb, for the aids to hearing, eyeglasses, and wheelchairs.

Sometimes when he goes away I am boarded with a friend. Once he put me up at *Le Toilettage,* but I hated that and got sick with kennel cough. He promised never to put me there again, so this time I stayed in our flat with Christophe who assists in the Sailing School. He brought me things from the plates where he took his meals.

He explained that he'd had to pay for the food he brought me because there are "jewelers" who come to the better restaurants and cafés early in the morning to buy what was saved from the plates of the night before—the uneaten wedges of pizza, the meats and vegetables and sweets that cannot be offered again, the melon that is more than ripe, the bread and slices of sausage that remained in the baskets. A chop only partially chewed is carefully saved for them. Only the fish is not saved.

The jewelers pay for these treasures and rush them to the bus. The food reappears at noon on the tables of the cheap bistros in Marseille. "Nothing is lost in commerce," Christophe said. "And there is a name for every assortment. The four-franc plate of yesterday's desserts—the remaining bite of this, the uneaten touch of *crème caramel,* the crumb of *abricot clafouti,* all of it jumbled together in the paste of red raspberry—it is called *harlequin*."

Jean-Michel's dive attracted many watchers. Collection plates were passed as he mounted the tower. He knows this is the best moment for generosity. It is a sort of good-luck offering from the people who are scared for him. He does not jump until he gets the signal that all the collection plates are in.

To help Martha replace some of the painting articles she lost in the robbery and to introduce Alan to the *bouquinistes* of the neighborhood—our used-book dealers— Jean-Michel and I directed them in their automobile to Marseille a few days ago.

First we walked through the open market in the direction of the art supplies shop. The smells there were excellent—it was the Algerian quarter—a pig butchering, food cooking. The waiters were writing out the *Plat du Jour* on their notice boards and polishing the glasses on their tables. I began to think of my dinner.

Although it was tucked away in a remote block, Jean-Michel found the shop without difficulty, a tall, compact space with room for two customers. Alan said it would make a fine bookshop with its old tile floor, paneled counter with scrollwork from the last century, floor-to-ceiling cabinets filled with paints, papers, inks, pens—everything for artists.

The proprietor has a narrow space behind his deep counter. His name is Henri Lafite, a man as compact and organized as his *Papeterie des Arts*. He knew his wares exactly and found what was needed as he is a proper French shopkeeper.

M'sieur Lafite's dog is associated with him in the enterprise. He is a gray terrier—something between you and me in size. His family name is Figaro, but he explained that since he is pedigreed his full name is quite long and is in the computer of pedigreed dogs in Paris. He showed me his left ear with the number of his pedigree tattooed inside. He is proud of this. The idea of it makes me wince. My ears are very sensitive.

So he is a dog of class, but that notwithstanding he is quite amiable. As soon as we came in he arranged to make our acquaintance. Since he works on the tall counter beside the telephone, to get down he uses the stepladder his *patron* keeps to reach the goods on the higher shelves.

I advised him that if it were my counter I'd simply jump down when visitors arrived. Figaro said it was a thing of dignity for him not to jump, but I think the real reason he does not jump is because he is older and has a touch of rheumatism.

Did you not tell me that you have experienced a stiffness in the knee that was operated after your encounter with Miste? Not surprising that you should know some stiffness at your age, Old Man! I too have a stiffness I notice when I sit down. It is a sort of catch in the joint. So I sit down carefully, especially in the cool weather. That is when it bothers me particularly.

Anyway, it being a warm afternoon and the air very close in Marseille, Figaro lay down on the cool tiles. I joined him as Alan and Jean-Michel crossed the busy street to the bookstalls. Figaro is accustomed to company. He explained that he welcomes visiting dogs but he cannot allow another dog behind the counter.

"For seven years he sleeps with me," M'sieur Lafite told Alan. Your *patron* said he understood, for fourteen years you have slept with him.

By the time Alan and Jean-Michel returned and Martha's goods had been selected, discussed, wrapped, and paid for, the fragrances coming in from the neighborhood kitchens were making me drool.

A most satisfactory dinner was laid on for us at The Palace of Couscous, which I would describe but it would make you hungry for the cuisine of France, and that would only lead to a frustration. Also, tonight I do not dine so well, so I do not want to discontent myself. Suffice it that the waiter is a particular friend of *le patron*'s. A mere nod and I was attended to. I like dining out.

I am yawning. Goodnight, my merry one. I think Alan will sleep well tonight after his big sailing voyage. For all his sea-sickness, he is proud to have gone out on *Zodiac* with *le patron* and Rodeo.

At dinner tonight he told Robert of La Caravelle about his sea voyage. Robert allowed him to wear the admiral's hat through the meal and presented him with two carafes of the fine white wine of Cassis in honor of his achievement.

"This wine grows right up there," Robert said, pointing. "It has its roots in the sea! This is in honor of your *Baptême*."

When Alan left Robert saluted and called him "*Commandeur*."

Then he asked for his hat back.

I sleep soundly for the six hours Jean-Michel sleeps. I am not wakeful. Are you wakeful? *Le patron* says that wakefulness is a thing of the conscience. He learned from l' Abbé Simon that if you are good, you will fall like a stone at night and rise like a loaf at dawn. Over and over he reminds me as if to remind himself, "Abbé Simon said in life there are two doors. The right door and the wrong door. Go through the wrong door and there will be no rest for you. Abbé Simon would pull my ear when he saw me heading for the wrong door. He was firm in his love. Now I can sleep."

Good night Jefe. Rest well. From what I know of you, I think you must have a good conscience.

Rodeo

September 18, Hatfield

Dear Dad—

Here is the map I worked up with Margie. She struggled to remember. She'd dug out her letters from Ellen. Did you know she went back to Germany in 1957?

Before they were caught and jailed, she and her father and brother buried the family silver and what remained of the jewelry in the back yard near a big tree. All the rings and bracelets they owned were sewn into her clothes. Even her parents' wedding bands.

She went back fifteen years later to collect what they'd buried and put up stones for her family. Her home street was there but no sign of the house or the tree. An apartment had been built over what must have been their house plot. The neighbors said everything had been bombed to rubble. No sign of the foundry either.

In one of her letters she told Margie how it had made her dizzy to the point of nausea to come to what she knew was her home place and to find it totally strange, its memory of her stripped away as if none of it had happened, it was another place, she was another person.

She bought eight stones. She'd planned to mark them with the names, but in the end she grouped them together in a row and had the carver write across the row, "*Gute Nacht meine liebe Mamma, Gute Nacht mein lieber Papa, Gute Nacht alle meine geliebten, Gute Nacht.*" No names.

She died in Milwaukee in 1960. She was 38. Margie said Ellen's stomach never got right after the War. She couldn't keep weight.

Margie remembers hearing that out of Marseille they were guided by a man with a dog that could not bark.

Hope this helps. Margie thinks you're after the buried treasure.

Love, Ben

September 20, Cassis

Dear Ben—

Thanks for the map. When I have the right opportunity I'm going to show it to the one man here who I think can help me. I've written you about him—Henri, the French merchant mariner who did a stint with the *Kreigsmarin*.

At last I made it out on *Zodiac* with M'sieur Beaujon and The Mariner dog. May it be my last voyage on that flapping, slapping overblown innertube!

At first it was calm. We all sang as we towed the sailboats. About a mile out the painter was disengaged and Jean-Michel rehearsed his sailors in tacking, coming about, leaning out as they came before the wind, full tiller port, full tiller starboard. They did well! He cheered them! The sailors were proud of what they could do.

To his delight and my dismay the wind picked up. There were swells and whitecaps. He drilled his sailors in running before the wind. He raced around the flotilla in *Zodiac* at full throttle, yelling like a madman how they should take best advantage of the wind.

Rodeo trembled and barked the whole time. He's amazingly steady, balancing smoothly as *Zodiac* pitches and rolls, but that takes footwork, and he trembles. Given the spray and the water we shipped as J-M careened the boat around, I thought the dog was cold. Now I'd say he was shaking with fear.

I was afraid too when the sea got rough. I petted him. At one point I was hanging on to him to steady myself.

I asked Jean-Michel if the dog was cold. "No," he said. "He shakes because he cannot get the seagulls. That is why he is barking and shaking. He hates the seagulls."

I think it was part excitement and part fear. He could go overboard at any moment. What with the motor roaring and all the yelling, who would notice?

Jean-Michel declared a race. He goes crazy when there's a race, yells like a madman, loses all sense of himself. He must go home hoarse. And Rodeo too. The one eggs the other on. What with the barking, the endless *"Allez! Allez! Allez!"* the coaching tips and all the "*Giddyup Ongawas*!" I got a headache. Plus I was holding on for dear life! I got good and wet.

To critique their technique and spice things up for his sailors, Jean-Michel weaves *Zodiac* among the racing sailboats. This gives them wake to contend with in addition to the wind and the swells. Of course we kept encountering our own wake as we wove around.

The sailors all yell as madly as Jean-Michel, shaking their fists and screaming at him as he cuts close. They must go home exhausted and shaking. I did.

To wind things up he made them do a barrel race—stitch down the long row of yellow channel markers, the *Zodiac* leading of course at high speed.

Rodeo squats down when the high-speed stuff is going on, but he never stops barking. I began to get seasick, but then I started yelling too and somehow that took my mind off things. I understand now why soldiers going into battle yell like mad. It drives everything else out of your head. I'm proud to say I kept my stomach and nobody was the wiser for my being afraid.

That night we went to La Caravelle. I had a bottle of wine to calm down. I told the owner about my day at sea. He put his yachting hat on me and gave us a carafe of the white of Cassis on the house. When we left he called me "Captain." He and Jean-Michel are friends. I think he'd heard I'd had a day of it.

Today on the port I encountered John, the *pêcheur* who sometimes works at Marie Laurant's.

He's a tall skinny man, tanned to a dark brick red. He keeps a dead stub cigar in his mouth. He speaks some English, which he says he learned in the Navy when they called at New Orleans. "English of New Orleans," he says, " jazz, women and Negroes." He has a tic. He talks through his cigar. I've never seen it lit. His mouth is stuck and his head jerks. He cannot smile. He drools a little, so he is always pulling out the cigar and wiping his mouth with the back of his hand. He was picking fish out of his net.

"How was it today?" I asked.

"OK," John replied, holding up a bag. "Since 3 A.M. Going to bed now. Tired. The fishermen of Cassis used to support the town. Now I cannot even support myself. I must work at La Poissonêrie where the fish come in boxes from somewhere else. Bad thing."

He flies three faded red-and-white-stripe triangles on his boat—the net buoy markers I wrote you about. All the fishing boats fly these high-up pennants, good luck rags like the ones the *boules* players carry. I asked John where his cloth came from. "A fine skirt I knew!" he said with a laugh.

You ask how I've found the bookshops here. A few days ago we drove to Marseille with Jean-Michel and Rodeo to replace some art supplies Martha lost in our break in. The biggest loss? Her Provençal violet.

While Martha selected her paints and canvas, Jean-Michel and I visited the *bouquinistes* in the neighborhood. The stalls looked promising like the ones in Paris, long dark green boxes at waist height, but in the ones closest to the street there were few books. The largest trade seemed to be in *noire* comics, old records and girlie magazines. The men standing around the stalls didn't look like readers. There were no women. In the air I caught the fragrance of the herb. Nothing for me to buy.

Jean-Michel walks fast. He was way ahead of me aimed for another group of stalls. These had books, leather-bound classics of the last century, broken sets, books of photographs, paperbacks, all in French. But one man my age had a stall marked "English."

This man was tanned deep like a smoked fish. He was balding, his pate weathered to a fine brown. He wore a good muttonchop beard and sturdy wide-wale corduroy pants. His shoes were boots really, reddish brown of good leather. His jacket was green velvet. How he supports his sartorials on his titles I don't know. They were mainly paperbacks, mysteries and hot sellers of the '60s and '70s with a scattering of Penguins. But at the front of his book box I came upon a small thing nicely bound in dark green buckram with gold stamping, *Maxims of A Queen*. At 43 pages it was just the right size for a pocketful of maxims, and it was nicely made— "London, John Lane, The Bodley Head, MCMVII." The inscription on the flyleaf was to "Louis Shiffon de G.F. Mai 1914." May, 1914! Who Louis Schiffon and "G.F." were and what this little book has lived through would make a book. It was marked 100 Francs—almost $20.

I looked for my man. A lady had approached with a bag. She had books to sell. A chair was provided. She sat down. They had a long pow wow. The covers were examined as they parleyed, the end-papers read, the contents inspected. One title I could make out, Pynchon's *Mason & Dixon*. An unreadable. But the books were just an excuse for a chat. They are old friends. She's a picker. Coins were exchanged, kisses, *au revoirs* and *à bientôts*. Then he could deal with me.

He shook his head at the price. "It is too much," he said. He settled for half and gave me a postcard of a *bouquiniste* of the last century sitting on just such a chair before just such a box wearing a huge hat. They were of the same girth. Perhaps my man has such a hat.

I explained that I was in a similar business in Massachusetts. He grew very excited, pressed his paperback *Soul of a New Machine* on me and said that we must meet in a café one day. Jean-Michel beamed. Then another customer came up and relieved him of the ponderous Pynchon. We three swore we'd meet in the café right over there the next time I came to Marseille.

Martha found everything she needed, and the dinner after was a success because we ordered for ten legs. The waiter knew exactly what to do for Rodeo. Dogs frequent the restaurants here. The waiter presented him with a starter dish of scraps from another table just finished.

Our *Couscous Royal* was served in two large pots—one for the yellow beads of pasta cooked with vegetables and grilled veal, sausage, chicken and lambchops—I drool as I write this—the other for the thick dark gravy and miscellaneous bits of meat and bones.

Rodeo is not a slow eater. He finished his first plate while we were still serving, and then he sat watching. It is difficult not to respond to the stare of a large hungry *berger*. A number of veal and lamb chops made their way to The Mariner's plate. He was not demure about the chicken. Like Jefe, he knew exactly how to manage chicken bones. At the end there was not one grain of couscous or drop of gravy remaining. It cost 250 FF—about $40, with two bottles of Beaujolais.

Rodeo walked slowly back to the car and slept on the ledge all the way home. There was no looking out the rear window. He is a large dog anyway, and that dinner inflated him.

There was no eloquence, but we were not at a loss for words over our meal. Jean-Michel of course handled all of the back-and-forth with the waiter, and as you might imagine there was a lot of gesturing and soundings of pleasure over the food, and we all had a lot to say to our dog. He was our interpreter. He did very well at it.

An odd thing this morning. We headed over to Presqu'île early. On our way we noticed a big blue hot-air balloon. We seemed to be driving toward it. We got to the painting spot and there was its launch trailer and escort helicopter, a toy helicopter it seemed until they fired it up. Women in khaki scurried around with two-way radios. We got set up. A balloon tender walked by with her two-way. We had a chat. She had her shirt way open. This is the French way.

"How can you bring it back?" I asked. "Doesn't it drift with the wind?"

She assured me the balloon would come back this way and land right here. But it didn't. It disappeared. An hour later there was a tremendous whine as they started up the toy helicopter, then all the noise and dust you can imagine and it flew away. The ladies left in the truck with the launch trailer. We never saw the balloon again.

This afternoon I had my session with our landlord, M'sieur Ducroux, going over Mon Beaujon's dossier. It was as I had imagined it would be, long and tedious with a lot of dictionary-thumbing. I wanted a general overview; I was given a strict reading that ran from lunch through tea.

Most of it has to do with fund raising for the *incapacitateds*. Very little is Jean-Michel in his own voice, but I did get this: "In working with the limiteds it is something to give them the means to hear, the means to walk or to move around. That is what the money is for. But our project—our effort—is to give them the courage to hear, to move—even a little. To break down their feeling of differentness. To give them a sense of their own possibility—that it is possible to hear something, to move somewhere, to perform an act. The smallest thing one can do on his own is significant."

I think M'sieur Ducroux now has a different view of M'sieur Beaujon.

To thank the Ducroux for their kindnesses to us—the teas, the run to Marseille for the converter, the translatings, the *apéritifs*—we invited them out to dinner. We went to the restaurant of their choice, Le Bonaparte, a small place run by an intense, quick man who parks his tables out in the street and rushes around like a surgeon between operations.

All the old men have stories of the War. The women, no—or they won't speak of it. But for the men, a few drinks and those are the stories they tell. Nothing else in memory is so sharp. Over dinner our conversation turned to the War.

"I was too young, too protected to notice it very much except for your bombing," Mme Ducroux said. "Yes, the Americans' bombing! To get the submarine pens. It was worse for Paul. He was nineteen."

I asked Paul, "Were you in the War?"

"No," he said. "I was not well. There was not enough food. I got tuberculosis. I lived like an invalid.

"I get impatient with scholars who come here and want to talk about the cultural life at the time of Vichy. There was no cultural life! It was a desert! We woke up in the morning, and the question was, 'What shall we eat today?' No one had food enough in his belly to think about art, music, literature. We were miserable.

"I think of my mother. She would look at me. It fell to her to feed me. How she managed, what it took out of her. . ." He choked back tears.

"My cousin lived in Aix. Every few weeks he would take the train over to see us. He noticed that every time he saw his uncle—my father—he was smaller and smaller in his clothes. My father lost forty kilos—half his body weight—and he was never a stout man! It was that way for all of us. But you did not notice the change in people you saw everyday. You only realized what was happening to you when you saw it on somebody else. We were all shabby. Our complexions became gray like tallow.

"The Canebière—in Marseille, that grand avenue that rises from the Old Port—always so bustling and filled with crowds—after the Germans occupied the South of France even that vast boulevard grew empty. There was no traffic. Every hour or so a single tram. There was nothing in the stores.

"Then the air raids began and my condition worsened. The tuberculosis moved into the bones of my leg. There was no medicine. I spent four years in bed. I am lucky now that I can walk, but you notice my limp. Before the War I was quite good at football.

"Do you know *Gone With the Wind*? That story of Atlanta is the story of what happened in Marseille—the bombing, the fires, the starving, the terror. When I read that book I felt comforted because someone knew what had happened here, someone had told. I was not crazy.

"I read it in August, 1944, when the Allies began their invasion of the Var. We were sure they were coming here. Marseille would be stormed—like Atlanta. We had already experienced the air raids—two hundred bombers at a time, in the morning!

"But we were spared. The Germans quit the city without a fight. They were afraid of being cut off. Well—'spared'—the city was a shambles. The Germans had blown up the oldest buildings around the port, the warrens. It was too confusing for them, they could not police all its tiny ways and corners. It was not the spying they feared, they did not like the crime there—a thousand years of drugs and sex. So they advised everyone that on such and such a date they would blow it up, and they did.

"You know, every American to whom I mention *Gone With the Wind* turns up his nose. Even those who admit to having read it call it a 'potboiler' or 'pulp.' None of the American academics who come here profess to know it at all—yet they are the ones who come here to the Foundation to write learned articles on 'The Cultural Life of Vichy.'

"You are one of the few who admits to having seen the movie. Yes, OK, twice. And I have seen it more times than that—I own the tape of it!

"For thirty years I taught literature. I do not know what 'literature' is, but I know that that book—those little black marks, those words—convey a time, an experience in all its color and stench and smoke and horror. And, yes, ambiguity. Because when you are lying there helpless, who is your champion, who is your enemy?

"After the War we fought it all over again. The politicians, the communists, the Gaullists. There were the trials. There was more killing. They jailed Pétain—cheered by millions in Paris two months before the *Libération*, jeered by millions after. He died in jail, that great man.

"There was Charles Maurras, the scholar of our great poet Mistral. You have seen the pretty house he gave his town, the *Bastide*? He was an intellectual, a writer, a poet, a monarchist, a supporter of Pétain. He had edited *L'action Française* before the War. In the same month after the War he was elected to The French Academy and committed to jail for life. He died a prisoner for his ideas, the thoughts he wrote.

"If you'd had any politics at all you'd had to sail very warily like Mon. Beaujon's best students to make it safely back to port. And if you kept to a course? Zip!"—he made the gesture of a knife across the throat.

"Nothing is true in politics. 'Truth happens to an idea. It becomes true, is made true by events.' William James said that. And he was no politician.

"But enough of this."

His voice had risen with emotion. Counting the fringe of tables in the street, Le Bonaparte is the size of a small living room at home, mostly French around, but they understood what he was saying. And the Canadian and the Australian who were there, they heard too. The restaurant was silent.

Le patron of Le Bonaparte stood by looking very grave with his hands tucked in his white apron.

Suddenly he waved his hands.

"*Le jet fuel,*" he yelled. "It is time for *le jet fuel. Jet fuel* on the house for everyone."

This liqueur is always on the house at the end of your meal when you receive *l'addition,* but he rushed around putting down the little shot glasses and giving everyone a taste of *marc,* the clear white fire distilled from grape seeds. Jean-Marie knew that something much stronger than wine was needed.

Dad

September 30, Cassis

Jefe Le Chien, Son of Chocolate Momma—

You have heard of Picasso? Today over *oursins* and the white wine of Cassis *le patron* and Alan had a large talk about Picasso, what an eater he was, eating Africa, Braque, the Greeks, the bodies of everyone, what didn't he consume? And always he was spinning, working, making. Even the bits of old wallpaper he hoarded, he ate that and made from it. He ate with his eys. His eyes were like lions.

They agreed that he was a revolutionary because he was not tied to the past. It is hard to live in a country where there is so much attention to the past. For most Frenchmen the past is so present, it becomes the present. It is like living in a museum. How can you expect something new to measure up? But Picasso invented his present. He had no question that he could jump higher than the past. He must have been a formidable gambler.

From gambling they got on to politics. They are both Socialists—spread the work around and let the pirates who resent the taxes go where they will. The countries with the longest happiness are those where the extremes between rich and poor are not so great. The mark of a poor country is the size of its coins. The mark of a rich country is the blandness of its postage stamps.

After their large talk *le patron* confided to me that Alan should be an intellectual. Here the intellectual collects a pension at La Poste and is given a rosette to wear in his lapel. To earn this he must think and write a little. No one need know your thoughts or read your writing. Once you are selected by the politicians it is enough that you fill out on the yearly form that you have done these things.

Your patron is curious about the *Résistance* here. He has hunted down the memorials. From what

I have heard, there was not much food here then. Do hungry men make good partisans? Do sleek ones? The ones in between? From the memorials you see—many more in Marseille than here—they were all young, but perhaps they did not shoot the old ones in the street. And women? I wonder if any of the *maquis* were women.

What is this about your eye? "The milk eye" as we call it is common with poodles. There is nothing for it. It is the seeing clouding over. It does not do to scratch, it will only infect. *Le patron* says this is part of your discipline, your path, your thing to be endured.

This morning we went to La Poste so *le patron* could collect his benefit. La Poste is on the town square. A large brown mongrel is associated with the organ grinder who works in the square on market days. This dog's partner is a big, well-dressed man. He does not look or act as if he needs that job. He probably does it for his happiness.

The man's work is to stand behind the cart turning the crank to make the organ's bellows go. It is a pretty sound, old French dance hall tunes. The old ones know his tunes. People smile and pause when they hear this jaunty music. He sways in time to the music he makes and sometimes sings "La la la" to one of his songs. Many passersby leave a coin.

I am not acquainted with the organ grinder's dog, but I have heard his name—Milou. He is part border collie, and with him the claim is true. He wears a tan sun visor and a bright calico kerchief and sits on a table in front of the cart. When someone drops a coin in the cup this amiable dog wags his tail by way of thanks. He is patient with the little ones who dance around and fumble to pat him and adjust his cap. He was calm this morning when a toddler knocked over his coin cup.

But then an Independent came by and raised his leg as if to pee on the organ man's rig. Milou lurched up snarling. The organ stilled. His master spoke to him sharply. The dog lowered his eyes. He was abashed but sadly wronged.

The Independent slunk off. Then the organ master understood what had occurred. He came

around and spoke kindly to Milou. He straightened the foolish hat and gave his dog a rough but tender pat.

Le patron says it is a thing that warms the heart to see a dog smile.

Tonight the organ grinder and his dog were on the port playing love songs and songs for children. The man was singing full-out this time. He sang as he played, and he had song sheets for his audience so they could sing with him. Perhaps this is something he has just added to his routine for pleasure.

Old ones and very young ones leaned together to sing—they are not so self-conscious about singing as the motorcycle boys and the girls that ride behind them and the men and women of thirty.

When his hurdy-gurdy stopped the old people rushed to put coins in the money cup. They begged this man to start his music and the singing again. Someone brought him a glass of wine. A sausage and a dish of water were presented to Milou. The organ started again.

Jefe—in your first letter you asked a philosopher's question: "Why do people keep dogs?" *Le patron* says it is a very ancient thing, the affection between us, not a thing to be explained by science. He told me with emotion, "Wolf and man have lived together in the man's room for 135,000 years. The date I have on the authority of *Le Monde*, the fact I know in my heart."

Affection between people is difficult. I don't know why, but few people trust each other the way they trust their dogs. People do not tell each other the things they tell us. That is because we forgive them everything and will die for them if necessary. They know that. It is the unwritten rule between us. Jean-Michel says this affection is like strong coffee when you are tired. It gives one spirit to do the next thing.

So, Jefe my friend—I lift a glass to you in honor of Affection!

And now to work! I hear the children. This is a spirited class from Aix. Even before they reach the boatyard now they start to shout and sing their school song in their high voices. I cannot help myself, I must sing too, for all that it annoys Mme Ducroux in her apartment.

Alan says Martha always smiles at the sound of my voice. When the M'sieurs Pavarotti and Domingo return in the spring I shall seek an audition!

Am I proud? Sure! What is wrong with pride? Here is a saying for you to ponder, my philosopher, something from an old Breton farmer: "I am too poor to own a horse so I keep The Horse of Pride in my stable."

We do not know *la morosité* here. *Le patron* says that glumness is an affliction of Paris, a mildew on the spirit caused by the lack of sun. Here we do not lack the sun. What we do have in the South is la *méfiance*—suspicion—which *le patron* says is unique to this region. He did not know it in North Africa. So there you are. Every region has its specialty.

With the warm sun of affection for you my Jefe, I am,

Rodeo, The Voice

October 20, Cassis

Dear Jefe—

A question for you, my American friend. For luck do you keep a horseshoe? We keep a horse's shoe. At the shrine of Mary Magdalene the pilgrims have carved horseshoes in the walls, big ones and small ones, hundreds of them. We keep a small one nailed over the door, the open end slanted down to let some of the good luck of the horse pour over us but not all of it at once. Where does this luck come from? Are horses lucky with you? Napoléon is said to have asked about one of his generals, "Yes, he won yesterday, I know that, but is he lucky?"

Jean-Michel explained to me the meaning of the horseshoes at the shrine. The pilgrims came to the shrine of Mary Magdalene seeking a special favor, a cure, the answer to a prayer. When their prayer was answered they carved the horseshoe by way of thanks, so her luck may touch others.

But what "luck" is I do not know. And why is she referred to as "Lady Luck?"

Last Sunday we visited that shrine which is at St. Maximin, which is not far away. *Le patron* wished to leave a token and hear the organ concert. He likes organ music because, he says, it shakes the bones like no other. A fine old organ is there, spared during the *Révolution* when many such things were destroyed. Napoléon's brother who was in charge of military stores for that region made the cathedral a food depot. All the religious ornaments were stripped out and most of the fine windows smashed, but he ordered the militia to preserve the organ so they might play *La Marseillaise* now and then to refresh their fervor.

A curious thing in that cathedral. There are tombs of white marble for the ancient knights and minor royalty of the area. Many show the marks of smashing and desecration during the *Révolution*, but despite that, the figures of the dead were so carefully carved you can still make out strands of hair and the fine lines of their noses. And at the feet of many there are their dogs! Did the dogs expire with their masters? Are they buried in those fine vaults also? Most of the ones I observed are small spaniels of the sort that accompany English ladies. Perhaps they did not know *bergers* and poodles in those times.

A tall, dark man works as the caretaker in the cathedral. His face is weathered, he moves slowly. He wore the old pants of a cheap suit and a heavy striped shirt that was not clean. He carried a fine white cloth. As I watched he smoothed the faces of the dead with his cloth as if he were their father, tucking them in for their long sleeps. This is his job, and so history turns: after four hundred years we have a dark Arab kindly dusting the remains of white Christians.

A ship of your Sixth Fleet is in the port today. It arrived in the night, large and dark. For those who did not see it, they were awakened at 6:30 A.M. to its loudspeaker doing your *Stars and Stripes* and then *La Marseillaise*.

There is no marking on her other than the number "50" on her bow, but I am told her name is *Carter Hall*. I do not understand that name. We name our ships with names to stir the blood—*Endurance, Résolution, Fortitude, Invincible* are the names of some of the fine ships of our Fleet from Toulon that have visited here.

The names of your ships are surprisingly modest, but perhaps it is because you have not had a Navy for the many years we French have, so you have not had so many opportunties to perform gloriously on the sea.

All day long your young sailors from the *Carter Hall* are ferried in to visit the port. In the afternoon they eat *les glaces au chocolat*, in the evening they drink beer. They are strong young boys with short hair. They are eager with their *bonjours* and reach to pat all the dogs. I think they are lonesome. Between their time of eating ice creams and drinking beers they line up outside the telephone kiosks to call their mothers. You may think I am wrong, that they were calling their sweethearts, but Christophe asked several of them, "Who do you call?" and each one answered, "Mom."

Regards to the black bookman from—Rodeo

October 30, Cassis

Dear Ben,

No idea when you'll get this. La Poste has gone on strike. A sign on the door explains that the postal clerks are honoring *la grève* of some other government workers who wish to retire at 75% of salary after 20 years of working 35-hour weeks. Not a bad deal.

I realized something was up at the PO when, on my way over I saw, strolling by the fountain, the rough-looking gent who keeps a cup for coins on the steps and helps the old and the mothers with baby carriages up and down.

He was walking slowly and smoking, starting and stopping, going left, going right. On a leash before him was a small striped cat. Where she stopped, he stopped, where she went, he went. It was all very natural.

"*Belle*, eh?" he said, beaming at his kitty.

I like the Poste doorman. He gives you a blessing when you put a coin in his cup. He has that gift. It is something rare to be able to give a blessing. Some of the black women I knew growing up could do it. To give a true blessing you have to be beyond needing a blessing.

I got one today when I gave him a coin for the kitty.

They've just lopped the plane trees that line the port, cut the reaching-up branches down to knobby shapes that will, if they ever leaf out again, shade the cafés below but leave open the sea view from the apartments above. The effect is startling, like the shaving of conscripts—all those pretty locks cut off. The trees stand like a row of gawky bare-headed boys, awkward and shorn, embarrassed in their new nakedness. In a couple of hours all the dusty, rich gray green was gone and the trees looked like winter.

On Sunday the Minimal Circus of Cassis came to town, a worn motorbike towing a red and yellow rattletrap trailer. A tapedeck aboard played Vivaldi. The trailer carried five wooden chicken coops with cats inside, several round platforms at different heights, and a cat-sized jungle gym. The operator was a slim dark-haired man of 30 in a black T-shirt and dirty tan trousers way too big, tied around him with a clothesline so the waist part extended up his chest.

He cruised his rig slowly up and down the port trolling for his crowd. When he'd collected all the kids he parked and let his kitties out. Each went to her own platform. One looked mangy. They were introduced, Mme Eloise, Mme Lucile, Mme Briget, Mme Eva, and the rumpled one. He talked to each performer privately. As he did so each Mme nuzzled him vigorously. He whispered things. We were very quiet. The kids pressed closer and closer.

He held out a hoop and Mme Mange did a tidy leap up to a higher platform. He bent down for another chat. She nuzzled him hard. He must have smeared himself with anchovy paste and catnip. She leapt to his shoulder. A word, and she went through the hoop and over the bar.

A small fish was produced from the tan pants. She took it in her jaws, jumped to her suite and had her feed.

And so with each performer: the chatting-up, the paces, the nuzzle, the leaps, tricks, reward, and home. All but the last, the plumpest. She stayed preening on her platform. He spoke. He entreated. Indifference. He threw up his hands and pretended to weep."You know how difficult it is to train cats!" The kids were tickled. They cheered the cats and the show was over. As he carefully collected his own rewards he passed out photographs of his troupe, *La Honte du Cirque Français* — "The Shame of the French Circus."

A *mistral* today, but Martha wanted to work out at Presqu'île for all she had to battle the wind. It is clear, dry and cool. The wind makes the rigging in the boats at Port Miou shriek like sirens. Pine needles zip through the air and sting when they hit. The doves are quiet, the magpies are making a racket, the sea gulls are playing, coasting and soaring. M: "The sea is covered with feathers, a huge pillow emptied all over it."

At 10 I walked down to the bar for two coffees to go. The place was fragrant with the cooking *plat du jour*. Alice and Jules, the café dogs, greet me as a regular now.

The counter girl was applying the steaming milk to my coffees when there was a commotion. A fat man lumbered in and said something to the wiry, short-cropped cigar-smoking lady at the stove. His head was large and brown, covered with silver curls. His face was thick and whiskery. He had no neck. In an astonishingly deep voice, a real Paul Robeson basso, he gave orders to the Mme. She was not concerned, the dogs wagged. They all knew him. He lurched as he walked, thrown off by his belly. He wore a taut and none-too-clean T-shirt pulled to its extremity, and dingy yellow short shorts. His legs were tan and sturdy, rippled like pieces of old wood. At his side there was a pretty little blond dollie of four or five who said her *bonjours* in a voice as high and piping as his was low. It was the Emperor of Ice Cream, Mon Papazan, come to collect an account.

Last night we had Henri over for *apéritifs*. He is the retired French Merchant Fleet engineer who worked briefly with the *Kreigsmarin* before he went into hiding in Marseille. He used to hike over here to see his mother. He is the only old one around who admits to having known a *Résistant*.

He looked every inch the old mariner, lean and tall in crisp linen slacks, a white knit shirt with blue trim, dark blue shoes. Even his gleaming gold-rim glasses had a spare, shipshape quality about them. In this region of brown-eyed men he is rare for his bright blue eyes. He arrived on his red motorcycle—and this man is 81!

We started talking about Rodeo, his work with the sailing school, his magnificent bark.

Henri laughed, "Oh I know him, I know all about him. My dog Seaman was his forebear!"

"You have a dog?" I asked.

"I had a dog. It was during the War. For all food was short, I kept a *berger* all during the War.

"Fish was not the natural food for a *berger*, but fish he ate, and rotten fish at that, food they would have given the pigs if they'd kept pigs in Marseille, but they didn't, so Seaman survived.

"Do you recognize my dog's name?" Henri asked.

"No."

" 'Seaman' was the name of the dog that led your Lewis and Clark to the Pacific and back."

"I trained him to take nothing from a stranger, no matter how hungry he was, how tempting the morsel. Too much was poisoned to kill the rats. Even in my home, with food in his dish, he was not allowed to eat until I gave the signal.

"It was the same with his bark. Without my signal, he was silent. He would nudge me if some-one approached, tug at my clothes, but he would make no sound unless I gave the permission. Now his grandson of many times over makes up for his silence!

"He was never on leash when we were out together. It was his work to help me avoid the smugglers and the patrols on *La Geneste* as I walked to and from Marseille. If someone saw you in the dark, he would shoot you. Seaman kept me invisible on my trips. Once he alerted me that the *Gendarmes* were approaching my mother's apartment where I was resting.

Suddenly it clicked with me: the silent dog that had guided Ellen.

Another Scotch and I steered him around to Dupuy, his friend who knew when the submarines were coming.

He said slowly, "Dupuy was dangerous to know. Do you read *Treasure Island?*"

"Yes."

"Do you remember the 'black spot'? When one of the pirates was planning to kill one of his crewmates, he handed him a paper with a black spot on it. Well, Dupuy was like that. He never handed out papers, of course, but just the same Dupuy doled out the black spot to his *copains*. Not that he meant to. But every time the Germans got close to him they got his friends.

"By '42 he was the chief of the partisans here. They caught him, took him to Germany and put him in prison for political organizing. It was a work camp. It would have been worse if they could have proved that he was a *maquis* or had done anything. As it was, Dupuy and three others were caught with maps. It was the work of their party unit to map the shore defenses.

"Dupuy was the only one to escape. A girl helped him. They killed two guards. The Germans published a wanted poster with his picture."

"Did he organize the submarine rescues?"

"I don't think so, but in his party unit they knew when one was going to happen and in which *calanque*. Somehow they got word. Since his fellows knew about the guns on shore and the shifts of the watches, it was their work to ferry the passengers to the submarines. That was the chiefs' guarantee against betrayal: if one of the men had betrayed, he would be sunk with his passengers."

"Were you involved?"

"I was not one of them. I had no information. I have told you before, they were Communists! I was no *maquis*!" He was not angry, but he was firm.

"So. Enough of this," he said. "I will tell you now of my cruise to Indonesia where it is very beautiful and very cheap to live."

That's where it ended. He's off on his cruise for a month.

Dad

November 1, Hatfield

Heigh ho Rodeo—

I have heard of your famous forebear, the mountain-crossing *berger* who did not bark and perhaps led our relative to the rescue. What do you know of your great-great? Are you not very proud?

Tonight we're back from Ben's apartment in New York. I'll be days getting the chewing gum off my paws, but it was worth it—the sights, the scents, the buildings, the *frisson* of money in the air, the women in their fall fashions, the exotic dogs to sniff, the cheetah on leash (I did not sniff her).

We drove down because Ben needed to collect some books and disks he'd forgotten. Also to check on things. He lives in the West Village, near—almost above—the Waverly Theater. His friend with the two cats lives around the corner. The books and the disks were not the reason for our visit.

At the start of our correspondence you asked me to tell you about my worst experience. Only now do I feel lively enough to tell it. Before, I haven't had the heart to bring it up with myself.

A young man named Ed, a Catholic boy very serious in his religion, was a painter working in our neighborhood. Alan encountered him painting at Ernie's next door. We needed some work done. When Ed finished at Ernie's, he started on our place.

Martha and Alan went off for the day. Eddie had command of the house, the keys, and the duty of taking me on leash. Because we'd become friends, he'd allow me the liberty of the yard while he took his cigarette and did his beads.

On this particular day I was following the scent of a rat that had invaded our mulch pile. Eddie finished his cigarette, did his beads, then went back inside to work. He forgot me, I forgot him.

You know how it is between rats and dogs—do you know *The Pied Piper of Hamelin?*

Rats!
They fought the dogs, and killed the cats,
And bit the babies in their cradles,
And ate the cheeses out of the vats,
And licked the soup from the cooks' own ladles,
Split open the kegs of salted sprats,
Made nests inside men's Sunday hats,
And spoiled the women's chats,
By drowning their speaking
With shrieking and squeaking
In fifty different sharps and flats....

My rat had come a good distance—all the way from Buddy Duseau's. I followed and followed and ended up in Buddy's yard a good mile from my house. I was hot and dry, a bit dazed from my racing after the rat. It was now the time when the schoolbus brings the children home.

I had drifted out towards the road. A young boy saw me. He called. He was a stranger; I stayed away. But with his friend he chased and caught me. I was too tired to run very hard. He took me home and gave me milk and cold chicken.

When his mother came home she was angry that the chicken was gone and annoyed that I was in the house. The boy explained that I was lost and asked to keep me as a pet. I was horrified. I was glad at first for her reaction:

"He has a collar, a tag. He belongs to somebody."

But then:

"Put him outside. He'll find his way home. Dogs know how."

It was dark now. The boy put me outside tenderly enough, but then he quickly turned around and shut the door.

I tried to follow my nose home. It gave me many signs and no signs, signs this way and that. I was confused. I walked all night. I did not sleep. I was scared and hungry. A German shepherd chased me. I had no *machismo* to check him. I tucked tail and scuttled off. He was not savage, he did not pursue me.

I was like the hiker numbed by cold: I couldn't think clearly, I couldn't make a plan. My pads were worn and sore. Nothing looked familiar. The houses were nicer than where we live, but none of them reminded me of houses we'd passed on the bicycle. I was befuddled. I snuck into a barn and went to sleep. When someone opened the door in the morning I ran out. I smelled the river. I figured if I could get to the river I could trace my way home.

I got to the river OK, but was home upstream or downstream? I figured down. I figured wrong. I must have been two days along the river. I ate only once, somebody's picnic remains. The muskrats I frightened left their meal for me, but I could not eat it. I grew faint and hungry. I knew I had to get to people or I'd die.

I climbed up the dike and followed the farm road until I saw a house. I went to the door and lay down. Nobody was home. Nobody stirred in that house all that afternoon or night.

In the morning a young girl walked up the road to meet her schoolbus. Wobbling and limping, I made my way to her. She gathered me into her arms. She cleaned and petted me as we rode on the school bus.

They wouldn't let me into the school, but my rescuer fetched me a carton of milk from the cafeteria. That was the first food I'd had in days! I lapped it up. She tucked me in a shady corner and told me to wait for her there, she'd take me home after school.

At noon she came to see me, brought me part of a sandwich from the cafeteria and another milk. Again, "Wait," and again I snoozed, and at 3 school was over and she came for me.

But now I was not allowed on the school bus! The girl begged, she cried, but the driver was adamant. He threatened to leave without her. With tears, she got into her bus.

"I will come back," she promised.

It grew quiet in the schoolyard.

I noticed a face moving in the window. A secretary in the office had noticed me. She came out and called very gently, "Here Puppy, here Puppy."

I did not run away.

She came over and read my tag.

It was a red aluminum heart, a proof that I'd been vaccinated for rabies. It gave a serial number and the telephone of the vet who'd done the innoculation, Dr. Hanson.

The woman went back to her office, got paper and pen, came out and copied down my tag number. She called the vet. Immediately he identifed me. We are old friends from many innoculations and many clippings. He is the doctor who neutered me and operated my knee. He is a kind man who would take trouble to help return a lost dog to his home.

He looked up my home telephone number. The secretary called, but no one was home. It was now time for her to go meet her own children.

She put me in her car and took me home. As she had a large dog, she left me in the car. She brought me a dish of raw egg and kept trying the telephone. Finally there was an answer, and an hour later Alan arrived and collected me.

He clocked the distance home. On foot and by car I'd traveled eleven miles to Amherst. I was on the other side of the river! Even if I had gone in the right direction when I reached the river, I would never have recognized my home area. I had never been off leash on the other side.

Alan took me home and bathed me. Martha very tenderly bound up my paws and brushed me. She gave me good food. My weight had fallen to 10 pounds, my pads were worn and bloody, my coat matted. It was several days before I felt strong enough to go see Max and tell him what had happened.

"My God, man!" he exclaimed when I showed up at his yard. "You look awful!"

He should have seen me *before*!

What is surprising to me is how helpless I found myself. How do dogs find their way home? What happened to my smeller? Haven't you heard stories of dogs who found their way home from a hundred miles off?

I think I was too far out of range. A mile or two, I could have picked something up and made my way back. But on the other side of the river—I was like Mole in *The Wind in the Willows*, lost in the Big Wood. And—I tell you this privately—I think all the turpentine has damaged my smeller. It is not as sensitive as it used to be. . . And, I am older. Nothing is quite what it was.

Of course everybody in Cassis knows you, but just the same, do you carry a tag?

I now have two: the rabies one which is required by law, and a special one that rings against it quite prettily and gives my name, the family name, address and telephone, and advises that for my safe return there is a REWARD.

Hard as my adventure was on me, it was hard on Martha and Alan too. They yelled themselves hoarse calling for me, hiked all the streets and lanes of our neighborhood calling and giving their whistle, driving slowly along the roads and highways looking for my body in the gutter. For days they patrolled along the river. They called the police, the fire department, they rushed to the pound. They cried themselves to sleep.

When that secretary called they were investigating an ad in the paper about a found black dog. But of course, he was not me. They had a reward ready in case he was. They took it to the secretary, a bottle of whiskey which passes as the universal gift here.

My getting lost is part of our family history. Many things are dated from "about the time Jefe got lost" or "That happened after Jefe came home." When the family is together at Christmas or a birth-day or on Mother's Day they gather me up and say, "Oh how bad it was when we thought we'd lost him."

The realities are, they will lose me one of these days. I am 14, Rodeo, not so old perhaps as the shepherd who guards the womens' wear store in Cassis, but I am the oldest dog around, and my eyes are going. I too have the "milk eye"—quite bad in one and moving in on the other. I don't do "chase" with Ben on the stairs any more; indeed, he often carries me down now, not because I can't manage my legs but because it's hard for me to see down. Sometimes I fall.

I am aware of my end, but I think the fundamental difference between us and them is their awareness of death and our ignorance of it. This is because they believe in God and we understand that we are gods.

You asked about my cat friend's name. *Miste* means "cat" in Mixte Indian. Abby was teaching reading to the Indian children in Mexico and brought the name home. Along with parasites that she was a long time getting rid of. She didn't find the cat there. The cat found her in New Haven, which is in New England.

"They'll be home soon!" Ben and I tell each other now. We plan our cleaning. He has written a list in his tidy hand of what needs to be done. We haven't done any yet. Just getting the furniture back in place will take some doing. Ben cleared out the downstairs for his parties. Things have happened to the rug, there have been misfortunes in the oven and the dishwasher is broken. The yard, too, needs attending. The boy from the gas station was going to cut it, but he fell in love. And the laundry! After we ran through the sheets, Ben took to sleeping in his sleeping bag. For towels now he uses the paper kind. You can imagine the state of things in general.

With A & M's return our correspondence will slow to the occasional exchange of cards, Rodeo, and then one of us will forget and there will be the long silence. Before that happens, I want you to tell me something. When you wrote me about your patron's gift of the dives, you asked what Alan's gift is. I don't know. You have been with him now for a long time, what do you think he should give?

Since you seemed to like him, here is something else from *Poor Richard's Almanack*: "What an admirable Invention is Writing, by which a Man may communicate his Mind without opening his

Mouth, and at 1000 Leagues Distance, and even to future Ages, only by the Help of 26 Letters, which may be joined in 585266267384976640000 Ways, and will express all Things in a very narrow Compass. 'Tis a Pity this excellent Art has not preserved the Name and Memory of its Inventor."

I give you that with a friendly nuzzle and my regards—

Jefe

November 20, Cassis

So, Jefe, My good man—

You have learned that I am descended from the silent dog of the *Résistants*! It was news to me and a surprise to *le patron*, but a photograph of the gentleman and his dog taken here in Cassis proves the likeness, for his *berger*, Seaman, also carried the black star on his forehead that I carry. Of course there is no proving that he did not bark, but all the same I am very proud.

Once you asked me if I had a pedigree. I was ashamed before because I did not know my origins and perhaps I did not have any, but now I will say to you, "Yes, I am of a line!"

Alan has told *le patron* about his discoveries. Some of the old ones on the port who know what he is after try to help him. Today he asks the name of the Free French submarine that was sunk off our coast in December, '43. There is no record. He will have to consult the archive in Marseille, or perhaps the one in Paris. *Le patron* assures him that there is a record someplace because Napoléon saw to it that records are kept of everything.

My heart went out to you when I read the account of your getting lost—your long wander, the failure of your smeller, your family looking for your body in the gutter, calling and whistling for you for days and nights without sleep. It is as if that rat had piped you away!

No such bad a thing as that has ever happened to me, and thanks to your Technique of Franklin I think I am now more found than lost, for the wife has a new fondness to me and regards me as her protector.

To comfort me after I experienced your distressing account, *le patron* found you on a map of

America. He showed me that America is very large and only a part of it is the U.S.A. We have found you at Boston. I am calmer about you now that I know where you are!

Have you looked on a map to see where we are?

It was honest of you to tell me about your fear of electric storms. Alan says he holds you tightly through the worst ones. Curious how comforting that is. When I had my bad splinter and Jean-Michel had to cut my paw, he held me tightly in his lap and I did not feel the pain so much.

My conscience is not easy that I claim to have no fear of the water. It is true that I pant and tremble with excitement when we are out on the sea, but there is also a portion of fear.

I worry that if we were to capsize, could I save Jean-Michel? We are often a distance from land. If he were injured or taken ill in the water, could I make a rescue?

Yesterday a new group of children from Marseille arrived—our last class until the spring when the water gets warm again.

They were loud and unruly, "tough little monkeys," *le patron* called them. I barked and barked, but they ignored me. Finally I had to bite the buffer at the dock's edge to restrain myself from snarling at the noisiest ones. *Le patron* grew concerned about my upset, so he locked me in the office.

Then he told the children, "You and you—you two noisiest ones—you are being loud because you are afraid. Is it perhaps because you have not been on the water before? Are you perhaps afraid that you will drown?

"You are correct to respect the water. It is dangerous. But you should acknowledge that your fear is making you boisterous. I have known boys like you. I have been such a one myself.

"You are not in peril. I will teach you what you need to know to be safe. You do not need to be afraid."

He showed them how to put on the orange life vests. They looked at each other and giggled. Even the two biggest ones looked smaller and more vulnerable with those on, their little legs, one pair tan, one pair white, sticking out below. They grew quiet.

Jean-Michel opened the office and sent me to *Zodiac*.

At the end of that first lesson—not a lesson really, a cruise around the inner harbor with the boats tied in a line behind—they sang their school song to us in thanks.

J-M then turned to the boy who had been the loudest.

"Do you trust the life jacket? Will you jump in?"

The boy paled.

A little girl in the next boat yelled, "I will!" and she was in the water and so was I. She was so small and the life vest so large that only her legs were in the water, so she waved and waved.

"Super brave!" *le patron* yelled, and soon they were all in the water, but only for a few minutes because it was cold. Tomorrow they have their swimming lesson at the military camp pool.

Le patron needs only a shallow to teach them to swim. He holds them one by one on the flutterboard. That is the first thing. They kick and learn that they can move themselves and stay afloat. Then the floating on the back. When they have learned that they cannot sink, the battle is won! From there it is on to the breast stroke, which is our favorite. Your head is always out of the water with that one.

Well, my little friend. You and Ben are cleaning in anticipation of your family's return, and I sigh at the thought of their departure.

Here there is no hint of my leaving. The Franklin has made us cozy together now.

A manly embrace to you this fine fall afternoon. The air has a rare spice today.

Rodeo

December 27, Cassis

Dear Ben—

We're almost at the end!

They pruned the cedar hedges along the roads, which gave a seasonal fragrance to things, then posters went up around town with a picture of a small fishing boat with a harpoon prow. It was pulled up on shore bearing a Christmas tree with a big ribbon around, a large wrapped package, and on a purple rug with stars draped down the side there was a stuffed bear, a bunch of grapes, a large bottle of champagne and a pumpkin. The colors were vivid. The boat was named *Cassis*. So the Christmas Market was announced.

There we met a boar's head close-up. It was resting without the rest of its parts on a counter outside the *boucherie*. Big, hairy, snouty, and tusked. Its hair was charcoal colored with some whitish ones. What a thing for Jefe! A pal and a toy in one. And after a few days it would smell. The ideal gift!

The stalls offered honey in special decanters, small decorated clay figures called *santons* for your *créche*, pastries, stuffed animals, pottery. There was a not very fat Santa leading a patient tan donkey around. She looked like Stevenson's Modestine as I imagine her, that noble beast honored in *Travels with a Donkey*. And a pen with two friendly dark brown billy goats, and coops for four hens and a fine rooster. They were all different colors. One hen was black, another a delicate patterned gray. The rooster had chevrons of bronze. They talked to each other in long husky sounds just short of a cluck. They were especially talky because it had flurried overnight and they were cold.

After the Market I walked up from town and passed a clown. I recognized him from earlier. I'd seen a ragged-looking man slouched in a café chair. He had a round-topped black hat. Beside him was a grocery cart piled high with stuff and festooned with paper flowers. I'd taken him for a bag man.

In his clown regalia he was standing on the port wall, his face painted white, a red clown's nose, his lips painted large and sad, his face spangled with gold flecks. He wore flashy blue pantaloons and a yellow shirt with black slashes. He had on the distinguishing hat and fine white gloves.

A dove was perched on a paper flower he held as he slowly moved in a sort of rhythm to the tape on his machine, some slow New Age music with organs and chimes. Every now and then he'd raise his hand and the dove would fly up, do a little flutter, then roost back down. She's tethered to his wrist by a short length of yarn. The cart stood by, a dovecote. An off-duty dove was in there. His whole thing that afternoon was his dance with his dove. Very slow.

A sturdy woman in a vivid blonde wig walked by. He bowed to her. She fumbled in her purse for a long time getting out the right coin. He had a copper basin on the ground before him, a tiny stuffed bear in it, paper flowers around. She dropped her coin in with a clank. He held out the dove for her to stroke. She did, smiled, and walked on.

There was nobody around. It was a cold afternoon.

His burly linen-colored Lab lay on a folded blanket and watched as the man danced.

It's quiet now. La Caravelle and several other places along the port have closed for the winter, their blue and white tables and chairs locked up inside, the awnings rolled up, the windows white-washed over so they look like dead eyes.

We've become regulars at a closet of a place behind the port, Fringale— five small tables in front of the wood fire oven. Family and friends occupy one table, a tall, handsome, short-haired old woman in good clothes and clanking bracelets is always at another. Her bracelets—gold and silver, broad and thin, jeweled and plain—run from her wrists to her elbows, like an African queen's. She speaks to no one, but her face is alert, her mouth always just at the edge of a smile. She is the kind of woman men and women are drawn to, an electric energy. I bet she can dance.

Most of Fringale's business is carry-out. You sit down and the smiling young Tunisian chef comes over with large glasses of kir, "On our house because it is a cold night." People slip in sideways through the narrow lace-curtained door, embrace and kiss the *patron*, his wife, their pretty dark-curled boy, murmur for a moment while their pizza is boxed or their lasagnas wrapped in foil, smile and greet us with a "*Bonsoir Madame, Monsieur*" and nod to the bangled lady as they ease back through the little door.

One stormy night we showed up late. The lights were on, the place was filled with people, but as it turned out they were not open for business. It was the owner's birthday party, but they made us sit down just the same, share the pizza, wine, and birthday cake. We all sang.

We've had a few last painting days at Presqu'île. This afternoon I was reading when a young man came by and said in French, "I am a naturalist, where is the sea?"

As the sea was right there—Martha was painting it, I was sitting by it— I pointed to it.

"No, no," he exclaimed, "the sea for naturalists."

I was reading Steinbeck's extraordinary *The Log from the Sea of Cortez*. Natural history was in my head.

"Is there one here? A special place? " I asked, with visions of rare specimens and near extincts.

He was delighted. He'd found a brother. He switched to English.

"We shall go explore for it together, the place for bathing without clothings."

The water now is 15° C, about 55° F, cold enough to shrivel anyone's enthusiasm.

Your mother has confided that she's getting tired of working so hard, every day Paint! Paint! Paint! "It's like being thrown into the water and everyone yells 'Swim! Swim! Swim!' and I'm out there paddling like mad, trying to keep my nose up, trying to get—where?"

We are cleaning and packing up, rolling the dry paintings into the big cardboard tube. The night of the full moon Martha stayed out on the balcony until midnight, drawing in charcoal the way the light was on the water. When she came in she said, "Someone once asked Matisse, 'Do you believe in God?' 'Only when I am painting,' he answered."

A week ago Henri returned from his long cruise. We took him to a welcome-home dinner at Fringale where he exchanged courtesies with our bangled companion. Afterwards we went back to our flat for dessert and coffee.

"Do you know her?" I asked.

"Many of us know her," he laughed. "She was the town madame. Only a few years ago did she retire, and then it was only because of the new mayor. The new mayor's mother put him up to it to spite her husband. Madame C is very well-to-do. Her commodity was never taxed."

I had your map of France with its bright red "Xs" spread out on the table. Henri looked at it for a moment, then drew his breath.

I told him what I knew of Ellen's story, starting with her arrival in our home in late '44 and her telling Aunt Margie about the dog that did not bark. Henri listened silently.

"*Alors*!" he said, almost to himself, as if he were gathering his energy.

"I met her here. I was the escort from Marseille to her pick up at Port Miou. She was in a work camp in Germany with Dupuy. She and her father and brother were there. They had protested the

Nazis' laws and the spoiling of the businesses and homes of their Jewish friends. Or the older ones had. She was just a girl of nineteen, but she was tough and bitter. They had killed her mother.

"Dupuy fell for her. Through friends on the outside they arranged an escape—Dupuy, the girl, and her brother. The father did not attempt it. It was not a clean escape. The brother and two guards were killed.

"Dupuy's friends were not really friends. He did not know them. They were directed by his party unit. He was one of the *maquis*. They were very well organized.

"I don't know how it was above Lyon, how they voyaged, but from Lyon south they traveled at night down the river in small boats. Sometimes there were delays. Often they had to wait at the rendezvous place for days without food until the contact was made.

"On the river above Marseille I met them at the refinery where I was working.

"All I knew was that my friend Dupuy would come to my work one night and I should help him. This message was given to my mother. She was very black about it, she knew Dupuy was trouble. Many mothers had lost their sons and husbands because of Dupuy and his gang.

"So for several weeks I worked late at the refinery. This was admired by some and despised by others. The German boss was pleased. I spoke German anyway, so I was something of his pet.

"This may sound strange, but I was not displeased that he favored me. I did not want to be thought of as one of the *Résistants*. I was not one of them. Compared to all the other evils I knew of at that time, communism was the worst. I would never be a Nazi, but I would never be a communist either.

"The refinery was under guard. I did not know how Dupuy would contact me. I did not think it possible that he could get word to me there, but I was told to wait there at night for his message, so I did. It was a guard on his regular rounds who told me when Dupuy arrived. It was that same guard who made sure that a blade was always spoiled on the turbine, so our work never progressed. You would be very surprised what a small network can do through little acts. And how many innocents get stuck in their web!

"So there he was with this scrawny girl. They were filthy and hungry. It was my job to get them to the staging point up near La Vieille Charité.

"The guard hid them at the refinery. It was now late, but I went very quickly over the mountain to my mother's at Cassis. I took clothes from her, all her rouges and paints, and my finest clothes. I packed a flag. I packed my pistol.

"My mother knew. 'This is something of Dupuy!' she spat. 'You, I will never see again, but he will flaunt on the streets next week thanks to your life!'

"It was beginning the first light when I walked back into Marseille. I still had nearly an hour to walk to the refinery. I had had no sleep, but I had eaten at my mother's. I took a coffee at a café—the coffee of that time was of ground up turnips and chickory—and mulled my plan.

"My German was good and I was the manager's pet. I made a gamble that he would help me in an affair of love. The Germans are brutal, and like all brutes they are very sentimental. The right story will always bring tears to the executioner's eyes.

"I was back in the plant before 7. My bundle I gave to the guard and instructed him to have Dupuy and the girl dress as well as they could. Then he was to bring them to me at my work with the story that I had wronged this girl, and her brother had brought her to me to be made honest.

"My mother was a large woman of her age. I was taller and thinner than Dupuy. They showed up looking like characters out of a play. The yellow gown my mother had worn to operas before the War was draped on this girl, cinched and bound up with twine, the front rucked up to drape artfully over her belly. Her face was gaudy with rouge, her lips looked inflamed. She was the village girl in trouble all right. Dupuy for his part looked every inch the country bumpkin out to avenge his sister's honor. His face was blotched and scraped from his bad shave, his hair rough-cut, his shirt too tight, his tie not tight, the pants cut off at the leg where they were too long, his feet flopping in my shoes.

"Dupuy had not survived so long in The Game without being good at it. As this carnival pair was ushered to me on the shop floor by the guard all heads turned. When he saw me Dupuy screamed, 'You fornicator! You maker of bastards! Now you shall pay!' The girl, for her part, in terror or craft, wept spectacularly.

"The manager was there in an instant. I explained all and begged leave to take them to my cousin's in town. I was greatly embarrassed, I loved the girl, he would stand by me at the wedding, would he not?

"At that there were cheers and some dark looks. I almost overplayed. I had not calculated how moved my kraut would be at the prospect of standing by me at my marriage. He now became the gallant, he would drive us to my cousin's in the *camion*.

"I drew him aside. I explained that this was a very awkward moment, I had much to explain, I had the brother to pacify, perhaps it would be better if we were alone for this little trip, of course he would understand being a man of the world with much experience in such affairs. So I rattled on.

"It ended up we were driven to the tram. Once aboard, I got out my flag and pretended that we three were visiting from Germany and I was showing them the sights of Marseille. With the little French flag which I waved like mad, the costumes, and my loud flourishes in German, we became invisible. We melted into the little streets of the region of La Vieille Charité, got the girl into the hideout, and an hour later Dupuy was tucked in there as well.

"I went back to work. Now I had my very solicitous manager to deal with. He was proposing a wedding gift of a ham. I chilled him somewhat by saying, brute to brute, that I was not sure that the bastard was mine, I had some inquiring to do. Immediately he was off on the perfidy of women and how he understood my dilemma.

"A month went by. I let it out to my shopmates and the manager that I was increasingly sure that the baby was not mine, so of course I was not going to marry the bitch. To all of them, I think, I was the bastard—the girl had looked so wan, she'd cried so passionately. Then I got word from my mother that I was to make a trip over La Geneste.

"I walked to Cassis and got my instructions. On such and such a night I was to convey the girl and Dupuy to Port Miou. But I knew the girl could not make that trip in one night. It might take two, even three.

"I allowed for three. On my return to Marseille I hid water and a jar of lard for the dog in a cave. Dupuy's men in Cassis had left a few tins and a bottle of brandy for me at my mother's. We would survive on that.

"The rest you know. It did take three days owing to a fall the girl suffered. The night of the rendezvous a heavy sea was running. The waves smashed hard against the rocks. You could not be sure the contact was there. Nonetheless, in a little thing not larger than a coracle, Dupuy and the girl pushed out from the beach.

"He was good, Dupuy. He managed the little boat into the blackness and an hour later he was back and the girl was gone. In her place in the boat there was a large radio. For all I knew the one had been traded for the other.

"A month later it grew very hot for him in Cassis, so they arranged his escape. He was betrayed. The sub that collected him was blown up in the *Baie*."

He raised his hands. His lips were tight.

"So." He was silent for a while.

"I loved Dupuy. He was my hero. Some thought I'd betrayed him. Some still do."

We embraced.

See you in ten days—

Love, Dad

January 5, Cassis

My dear Jefe,

We are quiet here. I sleep outside in the pale sun while *le patron* does his reports for the town, his accounts, the new dossier for fund raising. Some days we make repairs to the boats. There is always work, but it is different without the children's voices and the noises on the port, the "*ça va*s" and "whooo" calls rising in the mornings. There are no urgencies.

We do not sail. There are large waves. No one can walk the lighthouse promenade this morning—he would be washed away. The waves slap like sheets snapping.

Alan left this morning. His going has left a hole in our day. I have no spirit to write, I have no more to say. *Le patron* is quiet too. He says that every leave-taking is a part of our death. On the other hand, I wish you happiness in your reunion.

As you are a philosopher, I make you a present of this parable. It is from Sumer in the third millennium before our era: "The smith's dog could not overturn the anvil; he therefore overturned the waterpot instead."

You could not come here, but you have made a wonderful splash, clank, and clatter in my life! Thank you, Small One.

Please remember your fine acquaintance in France.

Au revoir—

Rodeo.

Epilogue

Jefe died about a year after we returned to Hatfield. His eyes clouded over completely so he was blind at the end. He was very brave. He was fourteen. Ben finished his novel and married the girl in New York. And except for the passage of time, which changes everything, everything else remains the same: the sailing school continues with Jean-Michel and Rodeo; Henri, M'sieur Ducroux, Robert, the woman at Xxième—they all continue, too. And the memories of the heroes, "*Les Résistants*." To all the teachers, to all who resist evil, *Qu'ils Vivent Pour Toujours!*—Live Forever!